Revenge at Wolf Mountain

Above Arizona's Mogollon Rim the Pleasant Valley war rages, and into its crucible come Garet and Laura Havelock, who dream of building a horse ranch and raising a family on Silver Creek.

But, whilst Garet is away buying horses up north, Laura is attacked by a brutal outlaw who rapes her and disfigures her face. Traumatized, she takes refuge at Rancho Pilar and finds an ally and confidante in Rita Pilar. On his return, Garet vows to track down and punish the perpetrator. Fuelled by vengeance he rides to the stronghold of outlaw Gus Snyder and then on to the spread of rancher Loren Buchard.

Now he must prove his mettle with gun and fist before he can exact his revenge.

ISBN-10: 0-7090-7910-9
ISBN-13: 978-0-7090-7910-1

Robert Hale Limited
Clerkenwell House
Clerkenwell Green
London EC1R 0HT

Typeset by
Derek Doyle & Associates, Shaw Heath.
Printed and bound in Great Britain by
Antony Rowe Limited, Wiltshire.

CHAPTER ONE

Garet Havelock rode away from the H-Cross ranch with reluctance. In three weeks he'd return with the horses, breeding stock to begin the H-Cross line – a long time for his wife, Laura, to be alone. He offered to get someone to stay with her, but she would not hear of it. Hadn't she crossed the desert by herself and fought off Apaches at Eagle Eye Mountain? She insisted she didn't need anyone to watch over her.

After Garet left Laura tucked her long red hair under the broad-brimmed straw hat and set about doing the laundry. Keeping busy would keep her mind off Garet's being gone.

Perched on a three-legged stool in front of a battered copper washtub, she sloshed one of Garet's shirts in the sudsy water and scrubbed it on the washboard. Then she gave it a healthy twist to wring the suds out and plopped it in a tub of clear creek water to rinse.

Laura caught herself scanning the knoll above the creek, seeing in her mind's eye the ranch house that would one day stand there. She smiled as she reached for another garment. Garet would build her house; he'd promised.

Though deep in her daydreaming, Laura still noticed the sound of hoofs. When the riders arrived, she stood at the front door with a long-barreled Winchester .44-40 in her hands.

The man in the lead looked as old and craggy as malpais rocks. A big thick man riding at his side held up a hand, stopping the others. When the old man spoke his voice grated like gravel.

'Where's your man?' he growled.

'He's gone for horses. Should be back anytime now,' she said, her voice calm and her face expressionless.

The gravely voice continued: 'I'm only gonna say this once, so listen good. You and your man get outta here. I put up with the squatter because I could see he wasn't the staying kind.' The old man nodded his head at Laura's garden plot. 'But when folks start planting truck, they're staying. This here is Forty-Four range. I came to these mountains before Cooley and before Clark. I made peace with the Apaches with no help from nobody. Nesters ain't going to take over my range. First thing I know, you'd putting up fences. Them Mormons is bad enough. So git.'

Laura cocked the Winchester. The click was clear and loud in the silence following the old man's tirade.

'Mister, I don't know who you are. But this claim belongs to me and my husband. It's proved up, and we won't be pushed off.' She held the Winchester on the old man's belly.

'She's alone, Pa.' The one who spoke was a dark, handsome man whose likeness to the old man was clear. Laura moved her Winchester to cover him.

'I'll ask you once, nice, to get off my place,' she said.

The old man just glared at her.

'My name's Loren Buchard,' he said, 'and this is my son Rafe. This here,' he nodded toward the thickset man riding beside him, 'is my foreman, Dick Blasingame. I own the Forty-Four. No one runs me off.'

Laura's voice was edged with steel.

'Mr Buchard, I'm not running you off. Any time you want to come over for a neighborly visit, you're more than welcome. But when you come to make threats . . .' Laura's blue eyes were like pieces of ice boring into the faded black ones of the old rancher.

He blinked. 'I'm not saying you have to lose anything. I'll buy your land.'

'Pa!'

'Shut up, Rafe.'

The old man tipped his hat to Laura, reined his big brown horse around, and led his riders away. The big thick man, astride a pinto stallion, stopped to stare back at Laura. He side-stepped the big horse as he looked at her, then raked the paint with his spurs and jumped it after the others.

Laura released the hammer and put the Winchester back inside the door. She knew the riders would return. She just hoped Garet would get back before they did.

As the May sun climbed higher and the likelihood of frost was almost gone, Laura worked the garden plot, turning over the soil and breaking up the clods. Bits of green showed in the grass along Silver Creek, and the mule deer that came down to drink early in the morning carried racks of velvet-covered antlers. Quail sneaked in and out of the dry weeds and Laura knew they would soon be followed by lines of chicks. She made plans to get some hens and a milk-cow or two. No proper home should be without eggs and milk. And there would be children.

The days warmed, and mornings came without rims of ice on the water-barrel. It would soon be time to plant. Garet had mentioned a store in Show Low to the west and another in Concho to the east. Show Low was a Mormon town, which made Laura uneasy. So she decided to ride to Concho for seeds.

Early the next morning she caught and saddled Mandy, her mare. With biscuits and salt pork in her saddle-bags, money for the garden supplies, and a canteen full of clear creek water, Laura clucked to Mandy and the lithe mare set out in a ground-eating canter. Still, the sun was past midday when Laura came to the hill above the adobe village of Concho. A mission stood on the high ground above the creek, and several buildings bordered a village square. Laura walked Mandy down the dusty street. In a clearing children ran about, laughing and shouting as they kicked a ball.

7

Women at the creek washed clothes.

A sign on one of the buildings announced *Provisiones*, and through the open door Laura could see goods piled high. She dismounted and walked into the cool store.

A man came from the back. He shifted the toothpick in his mouth and belched. Then the corners of his eyes crinkled as he saw Laura.

'*Perdon, señorita*,' he said, '*Le puedo ayudar en algo?*'

'I'm sorry, I don't understand Spanish.' Laura spread upturned hands.

'Perhaps I may be of assistance.'

Laura turned to see a striking-looking woman in a riding-habit. She wore her black hair pulled into a tight roll at the nape of her neck and a broad-brimmed leather hat tipped rakishly to shadow her sparkling dark eyes.

'I am Margarita San Antonio Pilar y Guerrero,' she said, extending a hand. 'My father is Don Fernando Alfonso Pilar y Aguilar. You *Anglos* call him Don Fernando. And I am known as Rita.'

'I'm Laura Havelock,' Laura said. 'From the H-Cross ranch on Silver Creek. I came to buy seeds for my garden. But I'm afraid I've yet to learn Spanish.'

Rita flashed faultless white teeth in warm smile.

'How nice to have neighbors. Let me help you.'

Laura soon had the seeds she needed.

'You must not ride back to Silver Creek today,' Rita said. 'You cannot get there before dark. *Por favor*. Would you honor us with a visit to my father's *hacienda?*'

'Thank you for the invitation,' Laura said, happy to have a friend after long days alone. 'I'd be honored.'

Rita laughed. '*Excelente*. We'll laugh the night away and you can tell me all about yourself and your husband and everything.'

'And you? You are not married?'

Rita laughed again. 'Me? Of course not. Who would want to court the headstrong daughter of Don Fernando Pilar?

The one who wears trousers and rides and shoots like a man.'

'I'll visit if you promise to return the favor,' Laura said. 'We have only a cabin now, but Garet will soon build a ranch house. He plans to raise horses, the finest in Arizona. Perhaps your father will want some.'

'Perhaps. But let's not talk about horses and business.'

The *hacienda* of Don Fernando Pilar reminded Laura of a fort. The walls were of native malpais rock mortared with clay and straw. They looked foreboding. Laura and Rita were met by a portly woman who was obviously in charge of the house.

'Please meet Señora Paloma Javez, keeper of Rancho Pilar and wife to Ramon Javez, our *segundo*,' Rita said. 'Paloma, I present Laura Havelock from Silver Creek, our guest tonight.'

'*Comprendo, señorita*,' Paloma said. 'Please, *señora, adelante.* Come in.'

Laura found herself standing in the huge front room with a flagstone floor and logs for beams. A mighty fireplace dominated the center of the back wall. The furniture was made of juniper lashed with rawhide and covered with woolly sheepskins. The walls and floors were decorated with woven wool tapestries and rugs of a kind Laura had never seen.

'Some were woven by Navajos,' Rita explained when Laura admired them. 'Some are from Mexico. They add warmth, no?'

'They're wonderful.'

'Margarita, *mi corazon*.' A tall thin man with flowing white hair and ramrod-straight bearing entered. Rita extended both hands to grasp his.

'This is my father, Don Fernando Pilar, the third generation of Pilars to live in this *rancho*,' Rita said.

'Welcome to our home, *señora*,' Don Fernando said. 'It is good for my daughter to have a friend. . . . *Perdon, señora*. But did my housekeeper not say your name was Havelock?'

'Father!' Rita gently reprimanded the white-haired Don. 'Give me time. This is Laura Havelock from the Rancho H-Cross on Silver Creek.'

'Ah. Silver Creek.'

'Yes, Don Fernando.'

'Would, perhaps, your husband be Marshal Garet Havelock?'

'He was a marshal. Now he just raises good horses.'

'Yes. Well, *señora*. The *Americanos*, the *Mexicanos*, the *Indios*, and the *Mormonas* – sometimes we do not get along so well together. Please take care.'

'Thank you, Don Fernando. I will.' Laura said, puzzled.

Rita and Laura spent the evening in talk and laughter, and Laura realized how much she had missed having a friend. Laura told Rita all her plans for the H-Cross ranch, including tall poplars as windbreaks, and apples and pears for shade and fruit. 'I'd like some currant bushes, too. Currants make wonderful jam for morning flapjacks.' Later she slept soundly, luxuriating on a deep feather tick-covered mattress for the first time since arriving at Silver Creek.

Rita had spoken to Paloma about Laura's desire for trees and learned that Rancho Pilar had slips and cuttings she could give her friend.

'As soon as the saplings are dug up and their roots bundled properly, I will carry them to Silver Creek with our buckboard,' she told Laura. 'That will give me an excuse to visit you.'

Laura tied the seed-sack to her saddle, mounted Mandy, and waved goodbye to Rita. On her way through Concho she decided to stop at the mission chapel. Approaching the altar, she genuflected before the figure of the Sacred Mother and prayed softly:

'Holy Mother. Please keep Garet safe. Bring him home to me quickly.'

Back at Silver Creek Laura planted the garden, carrying water from the creek every day to slosh down along the rows. She hoped the saplings would arrive from Rancho Pilar soon, so that she could surprise Garet.

Laura started her day simply, with coffee, sourdough biscuits, and honey. Butter would have been nice, but she felt fortunate to have the honey.

Laura rinsed her coffee-cup and plate in a small pan, and turned them upside down on a dishcloth to dry. She took the pan of water under her arm and went outside, leaving the door open, and walked the few steps to the garden patch where she cast the water over her seeds. They'd sprout soon and the Havelocks would have fresh radishes and chard instead of dried beans and salt pork. Thinking about how good it would be to have the early vegetables and how she would preserve the summer crop for winter use, she re-entered the house and moved to the cupboard where the pots and pans were kept.

Suddenly a strong arm was round her neck, cutting off her air. A rough hand covered her eyes, the fingers digging into them so she could not see.

'Don't move, you slut! You kick or fight, and you're dead. You're dirt. Shitty dirt.'

The coarse words seared through her. She fought for breath. Her lungs felt on fire. The fetid breath of her assailant nauseated her. No! Stop! Don't hurt me! She clawed at the hand over her face, twisting to free herself. Garet! Garet! Where are you? Live! I've got to live! But only guttural sounds of terror escaped her restricted throat.

The intruder wrestled her to the bed and flung her face down on it, pinning her there with a knee in the small of her back. Gasping for breath, she cried out in pain. He struck her a hard blow across the side of her head.

'Shut up, bitch. Just shut up and take it.'

The blow stunned Laura, and the attacker quickly tied her hands behind her back with a pigging-string. Before she could see his face he blindfolded her with a bandanna.

He pulled her skirt up and tore away her pantaloons. She whimpered, only to receive another sharp blow. She cringed, and he drove his fist into her left kidney.

She bit off a scream.

He gripped her shoulder, turned her over, then slapped her face – right, left, right, left. She tasted blood where his

11

hard fingers smashed her lips against her teeth. She fought to keep from making a sound; her heart thundered as if it would burst from her chest.

Dazed with fear and pain, Laura endured, descending through the maw of Hell while the man sadistically had his way with her. Then suddenly he stopped. He clamped his hand over her mouth. Wheels creaked and harness jingled. A horse blew. Mandy whickered.

Quick as a flash the man made two razorlike slits in Laura's face with the tip of his knife, tracing the tracks of her tears down her cheeks.

'Now you have something to cry about,' he growled in her ear. And he was gone.

Then Rita was there.

'Ah, *querida*,' she whispered as she gently pulled Laura's skirt down to cover her nakedness. At first, Laura cringed away as Rita gathered her into her arms, but eventually she sagged trembling against her friend, racked with sobs.

With the rising sun, horses boiled over the ridge and thundered down the draw into the ketch pens, a trail-weary Garet Havelock close behind. He and his two companions reined up at the corrals, and Garet pulled the counter-weighted gate closed and slipped the leather loop over its post.

Now Garet had top-notch breeding-stock and two capable and loyal hands to help him get the ranch going. Dan Travis was a quiet, hard-working cowhand who had proved up on Garet's claim here on Silver Creek, and Tom Morgan, a tall black man with a missing right hand had been Garet's friend since the two stood back-to-back fighting reconstruction blue-bellies in north Texas.

The three men reined their tired mounts toward the creek where they let them drink long draughts of the silvery-clear water.

'Thanks, boys. That was a good drive.' Garet rubbed at the

ache in his left knee. 'Montana horses will do well in this high country.'

'Wonder what's keeping the missus?' Morgan said. 'I'd a figured she'd have Mandy saddled up and be down here before we got these cayuses in the corral.'

'Well, she knows trail-driving's hungry work. There's probably beans in the pot and venison in the Dutch oven,' Garet replied. 'Let's go see.'

Morgan sat atop his rangy mule and surveyed the H-Cross.

'Havelock,' he said 'I gotta say one thing. You surely know how to pick a spread. This is one of the finest layouts I ever saw.'

'Sure is, Tom. But it's gonna take a lot of sweat to turn it into a first-rate horse-ranch. Still, with the Hashknife Outfit and the Forty-Four Ranch, and those army officers at Fort Apache, plenty of people'll be wanting prime horseflesh. This ranch'll be prime, Tom. I can feel it.'

Morgan grinned. The men pulled their horses' heads out of the stream and rode toward the chink-log H-Cross cabin. Reaching the top of the rise, Garet reined up sharply.

'Hold it!' he barked.

Something was wrong. No smoke came from the chimney. No bay mare grazed across the creek. The garden looked dry. Garet's eyes narrowed. He'd been a lawman for too long not to recognize the signs of trouble. He fished his Winchester saddle gun from its scabbard and jacked a shell into the chamber.

Tom Morgan shrugged his Ballard .50 off his left shoulder and across the saddle bows, where he held it ready for action. Dan Travis loosened his pistol in its holster and hauled out his Winchester.

The three men separated as they walked their horses toward the cabin. Garet halted when they were still fifty yards away. He dismounted, left his dun ground-hitched and dashed to the cabin. The others followed.

Garet flung open the door. The hard-packed dirt floor was

13

clean, as Laura always kept it. A plate and coffee-cup lay on a dishtowel. Garet's gaze inspected the room and locked on the rumpled bed.

'Tom, come in here.'

The tall black man ducked his head to enter. He paused, looking at the bed.

'What do you think, Havelock?' he asked.

'I don't like it.' Garet moved to the head of the bed and motioned Morgan to the foot. The rumpled bedcover was a patchwork quilt with starbursts of checkered gingham and bleached flour-sacks. 'Let's lift this spread together,' he said, taking hold of two corners. Morgan, managing the quilt as best he could with one hand, did the same, and they raised it from the bed.

What the quilt had obscured was clearly visible – muslin sheets and pillows splotched with blood.

Garet's heart leapt into his throat.

'She's hurt, Tom. I know it. I can feel it. She's bad hurt, and she's gone. They've taken her away somewhere. God damn whoever did it! And God help me find who it was. When I do, I swear . . .' Garet bowed his head.

Morgan spoke softly.

'She's a tough girl, Havelock. If she ain't dead, she'll be all right. You can trust her, man.'

Garet lifted his tortured face.

'She's hurt, Tom, and I wasn't here when she needed me.' A moan escaped his clenched teeth. Laura, his love, gone because he'd agreed to leave her alone, believing she could take care of herself.

He straightened up, swallowing hard to calm his fear and grief. When people broke the law they always left sign. He could read sign, and he knew when to follow a hunch.

'Come on, Tom. Let's get started.'

Outside, Garet said: 'Dan, there's blood in the cabin, and I think Laura's been hurt. Look around, see what you can find.'

'A light rig's been here.' Travis pointed. 'Buckboard, probably, pulled by a small horse.'

Soon Tom called from behind the cabin.

'Havelock, look. Horse was here for some time. Rider smoked, too.' He showed Garet a spot where a large horse had been tied to a juniper tree and pointed at shreds of tobacco and paper ground into the dirt.

Tom and Garet walked slowly back toward the cabin, eyes on the ground. The rider had walked that direction, leaving broken stalks of dry grass and an overturned pebble here and there. But his tracks weren't distinctive.

'I think he's wearing moccasins,' Garet said. 'No hard edges to the prints.'

Morgan nodded.

They found more tracks next to the back wall of the cabin, and Garet followed them around the cabin to the door.

'He stepped real careful, sneaky like,' Garet said.

Near the door two sets of round-toed boot tracks, one set larger than the other, hid the moccasin prints.

'Look,' Morgan said. 'The round-toed boots are walking backwards, and packing something heavy.'

Garet's face looked made of iron, solid and immobile.

'We'll just have to start looking,' he said. 'Tom, you go to Show Low, ask if anyone's seen Laura. I'll ride to Round Valley and stop at the Forty-Four on the way.' He turned to Dan Travis. 'Dan, I'd be much obliged if you'd stay and keep an eye on things. You might want to start breaking that filly to the halter and get her used to a saddle while we're gone.'

Travis nodded. He and Garet had ridden together long enough to make further words unnecessary.

Back in the cabin Garet folded the quilt and tell-tale sheets and put them in the cedar chest against the wall. He found provisions for Tom and himself and the two men rode away on their tired mounts, Morgan west to Show Low, Garet east to Round Valley.

CHAPTER TWO

Once again Laura Havelock opened her eyes to the darkened bedroom. She sensed it was morning, despite the dim light. A fragrance of old leather and juniper smoke filled the air.

In the days since Rita Pilar and Segundo Ramon Javez had brought her to the *hacienda*, the swelling had left her bruised face, scabs had formed lines on her cheeks like streaks of purple tears, and her bruised ribs now let her breathe freely. Laura's young body healed quickly from the brutal attack, but her heart remained deeply scarred.

That man didn't want a woman, Laura thought. He wanted to hurt, wound, humiliate . . . to make me feel like dirt fit only to be trod upon.

A light tap sounded on the oak door.

'Yes.'

'It is Rita.'

Laura forced herself to get up and remove the bar.

Rita Pilar entered with a platter of bacon, fried eggs, fresh salsa, and flour tortillas.

'We have no sourdough biscuits, *mi amiga*,' she said. 'Tortillas will have to do.' Rita smiled. 'I did bring your crock of sourdough starter from your cabin. Later you can show me how it works.'

'Thank you, Rita. You have been so kind. You saved my life. And now you want me to show you how to make sourdough bread, even though the tortillas are delicious.'

Rita smiled again. 'My people came from Spain many generations ago, and from Mexico to Arizona, though we called it Nuevo Mexico then. We are also *Americanos*, you see. And I think we should learn everything we can about you *Anglos*.'

For the first time, Laura laughed. 'It's a good thing my father can't hear you call me an *Anglo*,' she said. She switched to an Irish brogue, imitating her father. 'Sure and it's Irish Celts we are and we hail from Erin, the Emerald Isle.'

Rita laughed with delight.

'Come, Laura, let's eat. Here.' The Mexican girl handed Laura a blouse and skirt. 'You're larger than I,' she said, 'but Paloma wielded her needle. They should fit.'

'Thank you, dear Rita.' Laura used the tips of her little fingers to push the tears away from the corners of her eyes. But it was no use. They overflowed anyway, and streamed down her face. Laura turned away, but Rita caught her arm.

'Let the tears come, *amiga*. When you hold them back, the hole in your heart only gets bigger. Let them come, so the inner wounds can heal.'

'Oh, Rita.' Laura sobbed. 'You bring me to your home. You clean me up and give me clothes. But inside I'm so dirty. So very dirty.'

Rita pulled Laura close, and held her as she wept.

Garet watched Morgan out of sight, then turned the dun's head east. His first stop would be the Forty-Four, half-way to Round Valley.

Garet ground his teeth in frustration. He wanted to kick his horse into a run and push it until he found Laura, or the horse dropped dead. But his lawman brain overruled his husband heart. He could not afford to kill his mount, and haste might lead to mistakes that would lessen his chances of finding Laura.

The road swung north of a ridge topped with one-seed and alligator junipers. As Garet rounded the bend he could see the Forty-Four up a draw.

Loren Buchard had chosen well. The ranch was protected to the south by the base of the ridge. The buildings formed a rough U with the ranch house at the base, a bunkhouse forming one leg and a stable and tack-room forming the other. All three structures gave riflemen a clear field of fire all the way to the road.

As Garet approached the house he noticed a man with a Winchester on watch in the loft of the barn beyond the bunkhouse. Garet stopped the dun in front of the house. No one came out, so he hollered.

'Hello, the house.'

A bow-legged man of indeterminate age came out, wiping his floury hands on a floury apron that had once been flour sacks itself.

'Boss ain't here,' he said.

'Where could I find him?'

'Branding down by the sinks,' the cook said.

'I'll jag over there and take a look. Much obliged. If I don't see him, tell him Garet Havelock came calling. I've got a spread on Silver Creek called the H-Cross.'

'I know who you are, mister. You're the lawman that gunned down Juanito O'Rourke when he had the drop.'

Garet didn't like to talk about those days.

'I got lucky,' he said. 'Be neighborly if you'd tell Mr Buchard I was here.'

'I'll tell him, Havelock. Count on it.'

Garet continued on toward Round Valley, pushing the dun into his easy ground-eating canter. He turned east toward the sinks and heard bawling calves and lowing cows even before he could see the branding-pens.

A pall of dust hung over the corrals. Horses, riders, and men on foot were dim shapes. As the dun carried Garet closer he made out a sock-footed brown cutting horse pirouetting to hold a bunch of unbranded calves. No one paid any attention to Garet as he walked his horse up to the aspen-pole corral. A heavy man who looked to be in his fifties watched the branding from the top rail. As Garet reined in, the man threw him a glance.

'Howdy, Mr Buchard,' Garet said. 'Looks like you 'bout got your branding licked.'

'Yep, that we have. But this here is the boss, Mr Buchard.' He pointed to a bent, white-haired figure beside him, previously hidden by his large frame. 'I'm the foreman, Blasingame – Dick Blasingame,' he added. He slid off the corral rails and walked over toward Garet.

Garet turned to address the older man. 'Mr Buchard, I was wondering . . .' he said. Buchard gave him a sharp look.

A tall, slim young man with handsome features, black eyes that showed most of the whites around them, and raven-wing hair, came walking around the corral. He paused slightly behind Buchard, where he could hear what Garet said.

Ignoring him, Garet continued:

'Maybe you can tell me if my wife might have passed your spread recently. One of your hands might have seen her or something.'

Buchard swung a leg across the corral fence so he faced Garet.

'You'll be Garet Havelock. I saw your wife all right. She was standing in the doorway of that nester's cabin of yours with a cocked Winchester pointed at my belly.'

Garet's features steeled into a hard mask. Buchard's gravely voice continued.

'Like I told her, Havelock. I built my ranch from nothin'. I came into this country when there wasn't no one here but Mexes and Apaches. In them days, outlaw was something

19

carpetbagger bluecoats called all us Southerners. Forty-Four's got more'n fifteen thousand cows on this spread and Silver Creek's water for them. That creek's always been part of Forty-Four range.'

The rancher's eyes smoldered.

'Some'd just run ya off, Havelock, former lawman or no. But I'm a fair man. Your lady said you own that Silver Creek claim so I'll tell you what. I'll buy your spread, as long as your price's within a lariat toss of reasonable.'

Garet's voice was hard and pitched low.

'I've worked long and hard myself, Mr Buchard. I wore gray, and I fought with General Stand Watie's Cherokee Cavaliers. I've worn a badge, sir, and some say Garet Havelock's a man to reckon with.'

The tall young man standing by Buchard snickered. Garet nailed him with a piercing look. The youth's face lost its sneer. Garet shifted his gaze to the older Buchard.

'I'll not sell my land, Mr Buchard. I'll raise good horses there, and eventually good sons and daughters. If you want that land, you'll have to kill me for it.'

His voice polite but steel-hard, Garet continued; 'There was a time, Mr Buchard, when a man could run roughshod over a homesteader. But you can forget trying to take my land. It's just not worth the grief it would cause you.'

'But what are you gonna do without a wife?' the young man asked as Garet turned to mount his dun. Garet stopped, standing rock-still, with his back to the black-haired youngster. Buchard's son took a hesitant step forward, the sneer back on his face.

'You ain't even man enough to keep your own wife on your own place, Havelock.'

Spinning on his good right leg, Garet used the centrifugal force of the spin to drive the middle knuckle of his left fist into the temple of the dark youth just below the brim of his hat.

The youth dropped like a pig shot behind the ear. Garet stared at the rancher on the fence. Eventually he spoke.

'Buchard, if I were you, I'd teach that boy some manners. Otherwise he'll end up dead.'

'Rafe never could keep his mouth shut,' Buchard said. 'But that don't give you leave to knock him down.'

'Buchard, no one says a disparaging word about my wife, and no man makes light of our partnership. Him that does pays for it . . . your son included.'

Without a second glance at the inert form of Rafe Buchard Garet rode south from the sinks toward Round Valley. At nightfall he made a dry camp, picketing the dun in thick grama grass. He hacked away a few branches from a low-hanging juniper and crawled underneath with his saddle and blankets. The dun would wake him if anything suspicious came around.

When the dawn spread its gray curtain across the sky Garet's eyes felt like raw wounds. After years of wearing a badge he knew a man should sleep and eat whenever he got a chance, but when he closed his eyes he saw bloody sheets and thought he heard Laura's cries.

Becker's store stood apart from the outlaws in Round Valley, the Mexicans in Valle Redondo, and the Mormons in Omer, trading with all and favoring none.

'How do, Havelock?' Becker's voice came booming from the dark store interior as Garet swung down from the saddle.

'Not so fine, Julius, not so fine.' Garet's limp was noticeable. Whenever his strength faded he limped, despite the iron brace on his knee.

'Never thought of you as one that might not be fine, Havelock, even when you ain't.' Becker was a tall, spare man in spectacles and shirtsleeves.

Garet decided to trust Becker. He leaned across the counter.

21

'Julius, my wife is missing. I found blood in our cabin and I think she's hurt. Have you seen or heard anything?'

'Good Lord, Havelock!' the lanky storekeeper stammered. 'I haven't heard a thing. Missing, you say?'

Garet nodded soberly. 'I've got a feeling she's sore hurt, maybe, but alive.' Garet held the storekeeper's gaze for a long moment. 'Julius. I'd appreciate it if you'd keep Laura's being gone under your hat,' he said softly. 'And I'd be obliged if you'd keep an ear out for any word of her.'

'Sure thing.'

'If anyone knows where my wife's gone . . . well, Gus Snyder is likely to. I reckon I'd better talk to him.'

Becker lowered his voice. 'Juanito O'Rourke's little brother Luis runs with them in Round Valley. He's not a big man like Juanito was, but he's quick, Havelock.'

'The fight was fair,' Garet said.

'I know the story. Everybody does. But that carries no weight with Luis; he's loco.'

'Thanks,' Garet said, picking up the bag of supplies Becker had filled for him. 'And thanks for putting this stuff on my tab.' He strode out to where the dun waited. He took a moment to unroll the slicker-covered soogans behind the saddle. He took out a Colt Frontier .44 in a soft leather holster and strapped it on. He settled the holster over his left hip so the gun rode butt-forward only inches from his right hand. Then he put his soiled clothes inside the blankets, wrapped the bundle in his oilskin slicker and tied it on his saddle. He stowed half a rasher of bacon and some hardtack in the saddle-bags, retrieved a handful of shells and put them in his vest pocket. He walked around the dun, pulled the long-barreled Winchester .44-40 from its saddle scabbard, jacked a shell into the chamber and let the hammer down. He mounted the dun.

Garet rode into Snyder's town just after noon. He passed a row of dugouts built in the side of a low hill, then some tar-

22

paper shacks, before he reined the dun up in front of the two-story saloon with no name and dismounted. He left the dun ground-hitched and his Winchester in its saddle scabbard, but his Colt .44 rode high on his left hip. He touched the butt with the fingers of his right hand as he shouldered his way through the saloon's batwing doors.

Six pairs of eyes glanced up at Garet's entry, but only the bartender met his gaze. The other five returned their attention to their cards.

' 'Lo, Jim,' Garet said.

'Howdy, Havelock. You're a long way from Vulture City.'

'Seems the last time I saw you was in Ehrenburg. What brings you to this neck of the woods?'

'Shot the wrong man. But I'm awright. Round Valley's a peaceful town. Law don't come here, so I got no problems.' The barkeep paused. 'What brings you this way?'

'I need to talk to Gus Snyder. Is he around?'

'I reckon he's over to the house, just over that rise.' Jim waved in the direction of the rutted road. 'But ride careful, Havelock. Snyder's men've got quick trigger-fingers.'

The house came into view as Garet crested the low rise west of the saloon. It stood back against a hillside, two stories of squared ponderosa pine-logs. The small windows were shuttered in heavy oak that looked thick enough to stop anything but big-caliber buffalo guns, and Garet could see peep-holes. Gus Snyder's home was also his fortress.

Garet walked his horse toward the house, his hands in plain sight on the saddle horn. Closer, a man stepped into the road, his Winchester casually pointing in Garet's direction.

'Whoa up, mister. What's your business?'

'My name's Garet Havelock. I need to talk to Mr Snyder.'

'I've heard of you, Havelock. You was marshal down to Vulture City. Okay. Give me your hardware. I'll take you to the house.'

Garet had no choice if he wanted to see Snyder. He pulled

23

out his Colt with thumb and forefinger and handed it to the man. Then he plucked the Winchester saddle gun from its boot and offered it butt first.

The man turned and walked toward the house, Garet's Colt shoved in his waistband and both Winchesters in the crook of his left arm. He kept his right hand free.

Thirty yards or so from the house the man sang out.

'Visitor coming in.'

Men armed with long-barreled Winchesters appeared at each corner of the house. Both jacked shells into their rifle chambers, but Garet concentrated on the heavy oak front door.

The door opened inward, and a slight man with a receding hairline stepped out. He'd have looked more at home behind a teller's window. He wore no guns, and suspenders held up his gray pants.

'This here's Garet Havelock, Mr Snyder,' the guide said. 'Wants to talk to you.'

Snyder shifted his piercing gaze to Garet.

'Well?'

Garet met the outlaw leader's narrow, blue-eyed stare.

'It's private, Mr Snyder,' he said.

Snyder stood for a moment, then nodded.

'All right, come in.'

Inside, the house was dim as the shuttered windows let in little light. Pine boards covered the walls. Snyder closed the door behind Garet and slid a thick beam into place to lock it.

The slight man folded his arms across his chest, regarding Garet with a somber expression.

'Now what does a used-to-be lawman want with Gus Snyder?'

Garet kept his voice level and his tone serious.

'Mr Snyder, folks say you're a hard man, but I need to ask a favor.'

'A favor?'

'Yes, sir. You see, my wife Laura is missing. When I got home from up north, she wasn't there. I found blood in the cabin, Mr Snyder, and I'd take it as a real favor if you'd keep an eye and an ear out for any word of her.'

'Blood, you say?'

'That's right,' Garet answered. 'And from the sign I'd say someone carried her out and put her in a buckboard. Tracks looked like a man and a woman.'

'Havelock, I know you're straight. People up the trail say so, and Johnny Havelock's your brother. So if I hear something, you'll get word.'

'That's all a man can ask, Mr Snyder.'

'Name's Gus. Call me Gus.'

Garet grinned. 'Gus it is. And much obliged.'

Snyder lifted the bar to open the door.

'Give Havelock his guns,' he ordered.

The guide brought the weapons. Garet returned the Colt to his cross-draw holster, took the Winchester, and stepped into the saddle. He touched the brim of his Stetson with the barrel of the Winchester in a salute to Snyder.

'*Muchos gracias.*'

With a hint of a smile, Snyder lifted his hand. '*Vaya con Dios*, Havelock.'

CHAPTER THREE

Riding toward Valle Redondo, Garet again washed down his hardtack with good Silver Creek water. The taste of the water brought a flood of memories of Laura, and he swallowed at the lump in his throat.

Garet reined the dun up at the crossing of the Little Colorado to let the horse drink as he eyed the Mexican settlement on the far side: adobe buildings plastered with clay. A few showed signs of having once been whitewashed.

Garet dismounted in front of the low adobe with the word 'Cantina' painted on its wall. He ducked through the low door and paused to let his eyes adjust. The small cantina had only four tables and no bar. The room was empty so Garet took a seat against the wall.

A man whose face showed the tracks of advanced years came through the back door.

'*Sí, señor,*' he said.

'Got anything to eat?'

'*Sí, señor. Frijoles y tortillas.* My Maria she does wonders with the chilli.'

'I'll have some,' Garet said.

'*Sí, señor.*' The old man disappeared.

Silence hung over the room. Garet drew his Colt, cocked it, and held it in his lap.

Several minutes passed before he heard the sound of boots

– someone walking fast. Luis O'Rourke burst through the door.

'Hello, Luis,' Garet said. 'What can I do for you?' His Colt pointed at O'Rourke's belt buckle.

'You . . . Havelock . . . Murderer of my brother.' O'Rourke stuttered with rage. 'Now you wear no star to protect you. You must die for what you did. Now!'

'Luis. Look. I've got the gun.'

'I see it,' shouted the outlaw. 'I will not draw in here. But outside. Out there, in the sun, I will avenge my brother.' Spittle bunched like cotton at the corners of his mouth before Luis O'Rourke rammed his way out the door.

'*Frijoles y tortillas, señor.*' The old man set a large bowl of steaming beans in deep-red sauce before Garet, along with a plate of thin tortillas.

Garet attacked the meal with the wooden spoon provided. The food was hot, spicy, and delicious. Garet used the last tortilla to wipe the bowl clean and ate it with gusto.

'*Algo mas*, anything else?' the old man asked.

'No, my friend. My compliments to whoever cooked that meal. *Excelente, muy rico.*' Garet left more than enough coins on the table in payment. He pulled the Colt and checked its action, putting a sixth bullet into the cylinder before returning the gun to its holster.

The old man watched with somber eyes.

Garet stood back from the open door for a moment, letting his eyes readjust to the bright sunlight. He'd heard that Luis O'Rourke always killed in self-defense. If that were true, Garet had a way out. He stepped from the cantina into the dust of the street.

'I am here, Havelock,' O'Rourke shouted. He stood with his back to the sun about thirty long strides away.

Garet started walking toward O'Rourke, moving fast despite his bum leg. The half-breed gunman looked confused.

'What are you doing, gringo lawman?'

27

Garet kept walking.

'Get your gun, I tell you. You must pay for my brother's death. You must pay!'

Garet was fewer than a dozen paces away and moving fast. O'Rourke seemed frozen, his eyes on the approaching Garet.

'Get back, I tell you. Get back!'

But it was too late. Garet clamped a strong left hand over the cylinder and hammer of O'Rourke's Remington, preventing him from pulling the trigger.

'You can't kill me, Luis,' Garet said softly. 'Your brother died for the wrong reasons. Don't follow him. Live, Luis. Live. Don't let hate get you killed. Now I'm going to walk away and get on my horse. I'll leave your gun at the cantina.'

Garet turned away with O'Rourke's Remington in his left hand. He retraced his steps to the dun.

'When I am gone, give that back to Luis, *por favor*,' Garet said, and handed the gun to the old man from the *cantina*. As he mounted, a voice called to him from across the street.

'Señor Havelock?' A Mexican *vaquero* walked his palomino horse to Garet's side. 'I am Miguel Jose Pilar y Guerrero,' he said. 'I would take you to your wife.'

Garet Havelock studied the *vaquero* at his side. Where Garet and the dun moved loosely, ebbing and flowing, Miguel Pilar sat in his ornate saddle as if on parade, deftly handling his spirited palomino stallion. The four-inch rowels of his spurs never touched the stallion's sides. Nor could Garet see any indication on the stallion's sleek flanks that the spurs had ever been used. Here was a man who, though dressed as a dandy, cared for his mount. Garet smiled.

The sun had set and the last of the rose and coral highlights had faded from the sky before they reached the hacienda. And when Garet saw the *rancho*'s lights, his pulse quickened – he would soon hold Laura in his arms.

Miguel had revealed nothing about Laura's condition,

saying only that he was to take Garet to her. Now anxiety tight-ened around him. How badly was she hurt? Who was respon-sible?

The horsemen entered the grounds through a tall gate in the malpais walls that surrounded the hacienda. In the moon-light Garet could just make out the name 'Pilar' branded on an oak plank hanging from the crosspiece. A passage sepa-rated the big house from the quarters of the *vaqueros* and the smaller home of the *segundo*. All were within the rock walls, along with the corrals and the stables.

'Our men will care for the horses,' Miguel said when Garet looked around for something he could use to rub down the dun.

'A man should look after his own,' Garet said.

Miguel smiled. 'I assure you, *señor*, your horse will be well cared for. Come.' He led the way toward the big house. Garet followed, his heart in his throat.

Paloma was at the door.

'Señor Miguel,' she said. 'Surely you have ridden far with-out anything to eat. The table is set. The antelope roast is ready . . .' She turned to Garet. 'Señor Havelock, I am Paloma Javez. It is good that you are here. Please come and eat.'

'How is Laura? I must see my wife. Where is she?'

'All in good time, *señor*. First we shall eat,' the woman said.

Garet frowned. He wanted to see Laura. But he could not refuse their hospitality. He decided he could wait a few more minutes. They sat at the table and Miguel pitched into the food. Garet could hardly taste what he put in his mouth. Miguel tried to make conversation, but Garet kept glancing toward the door whenever a sound came from another room.

There was a quiet rap at the front door, which Paloma hastened to answer. A man spoke in low tones, then the murmuring voices faded toward the rear of the house. Why wouldn't they let him see Laura? Maybe she was hurt badly. Maybe she was dead. Maybe . . . He gripped his host's arm.

'Miguel, where is my wife?'

'Have a little more patience, *señor. Por favor.*'

Garet clenched his jaw. He knew he faced something he didn't know how to handle. Usually, direct action, fast and hard, was the best course. But in his experience he had faced other men determined to do him harm. Right and wrong were as distinct as black and white. Garet believed in the rule of law, others did not. Now he only knew that something or someone was keeping him away from his wife. He'd wait until he got a grasp on what was going on. Then maybe he could act.

Footsteps sounded. The swinging door pushed open and Rita Pilar entered.

'So you are Garet Havelock,' she said, striding toward him with both hands outstretched. Garet stood. Rita took his hands in hers.

'I'm Rita Pilar, Miguel's sister. I'm so happy to meet you at last. Laura's told me so much about you.'

'How is she?' was all Garet could say.

'I know you are anxious to see her,' Rita continued. 'But there's someone I wish you would speak with first.'

'But . . .'

'Come.' Rita led him to a small room lined with leather-bound books. As the two entered, a smallish priest in a brown cassock stood up from where he'd been sitting in a corner.

'This is Padre Juan Bautista. He lives at the mission.' She curtsied to the friar. 'He watches over our souls.'

Garet studied the priest. His face was benevolent, though lined with years, and his brown eyes were guileless. Garet offered his hand.

'Pleased to meet you, Padre. I'm Garet Havelock.'

Padre Bautista's gentle face lit up. He grasped Garet's hand firmly.

'Thank you, my friend,' he said in accented English. 'Come, let us sit. We have serious things to speak of.'

Garet sat in a leather-covered chair facing the padre. Rita quietly left the room.

'As you know, Señor Havelock,' the padre said quietly, 'your wife has been through a shocking experience. One that harmed her body, *sí*, but also deeply wounded her soul.'

Garet braced himself.

'It pains me to have to tell you this, my friend.' The small padre seemed to reach inside himself for some extra fortitude. 'While you were gone . . .' Again he paused. 'While you were gone, Señor Havelock, a man . . . an unknown man . . . attacked your wife. He struck her. He cut her, *señor*. And . . . I am sorry to have to tell you this?'

Garet felt he could not breathe.

'Señor Havelock, he violated your wife. With force, and with brutality.'

'My God,' Garet murmured. 'Oh, dear God.' He bowed his head and covered his ears with his hands. 'Who did it?' The words grated from between Garet's clenched teeth. His heart burned with the unbridled hate. Flames of anger rose in his eyes. 'I'll kill him!'

'I understand your anger, Señor Havelock. And truly, under God's law, such a brute has no claim to life.'

'Who was it, Padre? Who?'

The padre shook his head. The hard muscles of Garet's jaw rippled, and the priest held up a placating hand.

'I will not preach to you,' he said. 'But at this moment, your wife needs help to recover from her ordeal. It will take much time, and she may never be the woman you think you know. Above all, we must try to help her.'

Garet could only glare at this . . . this pompous know-it-all priest.

'Will you help me to help her, Señor Havelock?' the priest asked solemnly.

Of course he would do anything to help Laura. But the day would come when he would find out who did it, when he would be judge and jury, and the fiend who had violated Laura would get what he deserved.

'I'll help any way I can,' he said.

The priest sighed.

'Good. Let us embark on a long and difficult road.' He stood and beckoned for Garet to follow. 'We'll go now to your wife.'

CHAPTER FOUR

A candle flickered fitfully as Laura lay staring at the dark ceiling. Unable to sleep in the bed, she often curled up on the juniper-and-rawhide couch, preferring the feel of its feather-stuffed pillows and woolen Navajo rug.

She heard the murmur of voices. One sounded like Padre Juan Bautista. Several times the padre had talked to her. Always he counseled her to trust in Christ. But though Laura, as a child, often went to mass with her mother, and the soft-spoken padre comforted her, she could not find the courage to go to confession. She felt her sin too great.

She listened intently as the voices faded. Moments later she heard a sound that brought her upright, her eyes wide in the feeble light.

Garet! His voice moved her almost beyond endurance. She began to tremble. Tears streamed over the scabs on her cheeks.

'Oh, Garet, no.' she sobbed. 'No. No. No.' Clasping her arms about herself to stop the shivering, she huddled in the flickering candlelight.

Garet followed the padre into the dark hallway. The walls of the hacienda were thick adobe, plastered over with clay and whitewashed. Garet absently touched his fingers to the rough wall. He'd seen forts not nearly as solid as this house.

Candles on wall-sconces lit the way along the hallway,

where doors opened into bedrooms in this far end of the hacienda. Rita Pilar waited near a massive, iron-strapped oak door. Loopholes in the door and more in the walls on either side indicated this was the refuge of last resort, where *vaqueros* and their families would make a last stand if raiders overwhelmed the hacienda.

'I think she sleeps,' Rita whispered. 'Do you wish to disturb her, Señor?'

Garet searched the padre's face, then looked at Rita. Neither gave a hint of what they thought he should do.

He nodded, and the padre and Rita stepped back from the door. Garet raised his hand, knuckles toward the door. Holding it aloft for a moment, he took a deep breath, then rapped.

The soft answer came immediately. 'Who is it?'

'Laura? Honey? It's me.'

Silence.

He rapped again. 'Laura?'

Through the thick wood he heard a stifled sob. His heart went out Laura. He wanted nothing more than to hold her in his arms and brush the tears from her cheeks. It seemed like months since he'd ridden north, leaving her alone . . . vulnerable to the savage attack. Garet's own torn heart nearly broke his composure, but he steadied himself. Still, his voice cracked when he said her name again.

'Laura. Open the door. I'm here now. Nobody'll ever hurt you again, Laura. I swear. Open the door, honey.' He stood in silence for a moment, then spoke one more word: 'Please.'

'Oh, Garet,' Laura murmured so softly that only Garet could hear her. 'I love you so. But please. Please don't make me open the door right now. I'm scarred, Garet. I'm ugly. I'm not the Laura you love anymore. I'm someone else. Someone you've never met.'

Garet stood silently, listening to the grief in his wife's voice.

'Forgive me, Garet,' Laura continued. 'Forgive me, but I

34

can never go back to that cabin on Silver Creek, ever. And dear, dear Garet, I can't stand to see you face to face the way I am now.'

'But Laura. You and I are one,' Garet pleaded. 'Your hurts are mine, love, and we've got to heal them together.' He forgot that others stood listening. He thought only of his dear, wounded Laura. He tried the door. It was barred.

'I can't open the door, Garet. Forgive me, and please know I still love you. It's just that . . .' Sobs came again from that room of last resort. 'It's just that I'm not strong enough to do it right now. Please, Garet. Please let me heal a little more. But come back soon, so I can hear your dear voice again.'

Garet leaned his forehead against the door. Then he straightened up, seizing upon something Laura had said, something he could do to make things better for her.

'All right,' he said, his voice now steady. 'I'm riding for Silver Creek. But after I've done what I have to do, I'll be back, Laura. I'll always come back. I only leave you now, because I know you are safe in this room, in this house with the Pilars.' After another moment he whispered, '*Adios*, my love.'

Garet turned to the waiting Mexicans. 'She isn't ready to see me yet,' he said. 'I must do something at Silver Creek.'

Miguel lent Garet a blood-red bay mare with an off-centered star on her forehead and black stockings on her feet. She let Garet mount from the off side, and she had bottom and a friendly gait. Keeping her at an easy canter interspersed with walking, Garet reached Silver Creek in the still of early dawn. Across the flats north of the creek the dark shapes of juniper trees hunched against the silvery green of grama grass like grazing buffalo. Smoke drifted from the cabin's stone chimney. Dan Travis and Tom Morgan came sleepily from the cabin when Garet rode up.

'Howdy, Havelock.'

'Howdy, boys.' Garet decided to tell them what he could.

'Laura's going to be all right,' he said. 'She's at the Pilar *rancho* just past Concho. But she's been hurt pretty bad, body and soul, and she won't be coming home for a while.'

Dan Travis looked stricken.

'You mean somebody. . . ?' Tom stood huge and black and unmoving. His eyes searched Garet's face.

'A man attacked my wife.' The words grated from between Garet's clenched teeth. 'I aim to find that man and give him his due. I'd appreciate your help.'

Morgan nodded, shifting his Ballard .50.

'Dan. Tom. Help me pull everything out of the cabin and put it in the shed,' Garet said. 'I'm gonna burn the cabin down. Time to start work on a real house for this spread.'

When the household effects and Laura's personal things were stacked in the shed, leaving only the bed and bedding and the blood-stained rug to burn with the cabin, Garet got a jug of coal-oil from the wagon and sloshed it around on the dry logs. He struck a lucifer and threw it at the coal-oil. Fire flared, and in moments pitch started oozing from the logs, feeding the flames and turning the cabin Laura feared into smoke and ashes.

The column of smoke drew onlookers. The first came over the north-west rise. They rode four abreast, cowboys by their shotgun chaps and coiled lariats; fighting men by the way their sixguns rode easy to the hand. Garet Havelock stepped out to meet them, followed by Morgan and Travis.

A big man with rounded shoulders and a deep scowl spoke.

'Can anyone join the party, or is it private like?'

Garet answered casually.

'Kind of you to ask, neighbor. I'm Garet Havelock and these here are my friends, Tom Morgan and Dan Travis.' He stood expectantly, waiting for the riders to identify themselves.

'I be Max Baker,' the big man said gruffly. 'These waddies ride with me for the Hashknife Outfit.'

The sound of pounding hoots interrupted, and moments later, Johnny Havelock hauled his sweat-soaked roan to a stop in front of the burning cabin.

'Damn, Garet. When you burn trash you should do it a little at a time. Then a body wouldn't figure Apaches had lit fire to your place.'

The younger Havelock came to stand at his brother's side.

'Howdy, Kid,' he said to one of the cowboys.

The youth nodded his head, but said nothing.

'Seeing as there ain't no trouble, we'll be moving along,' Baker said. 'Come on, fellers.' He sawed his horse around, and the four loped back the way they'd come, leaving a cloud of dust to mark their trail.

'You watch those men, Garet,' Johnny cautioned.

'Said they were Hashknife riders.'

'Maybe so, but in Texas that kid's a wanted man. And Max Baker's got a reputation for liking to beat on people.' Johnny pushed his hat back on his head. 'Looks like you'll be tending that fire for a while. Think I'll take me a dip in the creek. Had me a dusty ride from El Paso.' He grinned at Garet. 'I'm here now, big brother. Don't you worry about a thing.'

The second curious group was Forty-Four riders led by Loren Buchard. They came hard and brought their horses to hopping stiff-legged stops at the edge of the cabin's clearing.

'See you took my advice,' Buchard said. 'But you didn't need to burn that cabin, Havelock. Forty-Four could of used it as a line shack.'

Johnny Havelock moved off to the left. Tom Morgan, his Ballard .50 on its shoulder strap, sidled to the right, taking Dan Travis with him. In a moment, Garet's friends were thirty feet away, facing the bunched-up Forty-Four riders.

Rafe Buchard edged his horse up alongside his father's big black.

'I don't see no woman, Pa,' he said. 'Five'll get you ten he never found his wife. Bet she's lit a shuck. Bet she figures

Silver Creek's no place for her.'

'Buchard!' Garet's voice cracked like a pistol shot. The rancher's fingers tightened on the reins.

Garet's every word was edged with flint. 'I told you before, Buchard. Whoever says something about Laura's saying the same thing about me. Now I find your boy insulting.' His face hardened down a notch as his eyes bored into young Rafe Buchard, but his words were for the old man.

'Listen careful, Buchard, because I'm only gonna say this once. A man attacked my wife in my cabin while I was gone. Now you think about that.' Garet gripped Rafe Buchard's horse by the reins just below the bit. 'If there's one thing a man don't do, it's harm a woman.'

Buchard grimaced. 'Sorry to hear about your missus, Havelock,' he said. 'If I hear anything, you'll be the first to know. Only the lowest kind of varmint would hurt a woman.'

'I made me a vow, Buchard. I'm gonna find the man who hurt my wife. And when I do, he'll wish he'd never seen daylight.'

Garet's eyes went from son to father and back. The younger man flinched as Garet released his grip on the reins.

'Too bad your boy don't have the courtesy of his pa. With his lack of common sense, he'll die young, mark my word.'

'He's got failings,' Buchard said. 'But since his ma died, he's all the kin I got. The day will come when the Forty-Four is his. Hope to God he's ready.'

Loren Buchard studied the backs of his hands clasped over the saddle horn. Then he looked Garet in the eye. 'You need any help, Havelock, you just let me know. We're neighbors. We'll help. You've met my foreman, Dick Blasingame,' he said, inclining his head at the big thick man. 'You need something and I'm not around, you ask for Blas.'

Garet raised an eyebrow at Buchard's change of tone. Two days ago he'd been trying to force Garet to sell the H-Cross. Now he was offering help.

'We'll make out,' Garet said.

Buchard nodded and reined his mount away. The riders followed, with Rafe Buchard seeking safety in the middle of the group.

Johnny Havelock came to stand shoulder to shoulder with his brother as they watched the Forty-Four riders out of sight.

'Wanna tell me what happened?'

As the dust raised by the Forty-Four bunch settled, Garet told his brother everything.

'Laura's a tough girl, Garet. Give her some time. She'll come out of it.'

'I can only hope. But this much is for sure. I'll find the man that hurt her, and I'll build her a proper house.' Garet fell silent again, watching as the sun fringed the clouds with gold before sinking over the Mogollon Rim, leaving the land in shades of blue. A heap of ashes and glowing coals marked the cabin-site.

Later, as the four men sat around a small camp-fire, tin cups of coffee in hand, an owl sounded its query from the brush along the creek. Tom Morgan grinned, his teeth shining in the dark.

'We got company,' he said. He echoed the owl's hoot.

At that moment a Jicarilla Apache, clad in knee-high moccasins, breech-clout, buckskin shirt and red flannel head-band walked into the circle of light.

'This here's Chiwadne,' Morgan said. 'Chief Puma sent him, I reckon. He always was the best tracker when I lived with that tribe.'

'How'd Puma know to send him?' Garet asked.

Morgan grinned. 'I sent up a little smoke the other day.'

'Like you sent that telegram to me?' Johnny's face wore a bemused look.

Garet extended his hand to the Apache, who clasped the hand and pumped it several times, saying something in his own tongue.

Morgan translated. 'He vows to help Iron Knee get revenge. Chief Puma says not to come home till the skunk turd who hurt Laura is found.'

'We don't have much grub, but you're welcome,' Garet said. Again Morgan conveyed the message.

The Indian pulled two cottontail rabbits from a pouch that hung from his shoulder.

Chiwadne stayed until the rabbits were cooked and eaten, followed by crushed hardtack softened with hot water and covered with molasses. He even took a second helping of the sweet. Then he moved to a spot some distance from the fire.

'Chiwadne wants to sleep away from the fire,' Morgan explained. 'He can hear better that way, he says.'

Garet and Johnny exchanged glances. They'd have done the same.

'Come morning,' Garet said, 'I'd appreciate it, Johnny, if you'd ride into Holbrook for tools. Tom, you can show Chiwadne the horse-tracks. I'll start marking off the place where the house will stand. Travis, I'd like you to keep working with those horses. Now I'm gonna get some sleep. Been a long day.'

But lying on his bedroll, his head on his saddle, Garet found that sleep wouldn't come. The moonless sky above was black-blue, and the stars were hard points of light that seemed close enough to grasp with an outstretched hand. But Garet saw none of their beauty. His mind reviewed what Padre Juan Bautista had told him. He heard again Laura's soft voice. This time he realized the voice didn't have Laura's old confidence. It'd been a frail voice, a trembling voice, a voice filled with dread and despair.

Tears welled in Garet's eyes and trickled down his weathered face. His soul ached.

Long after the others lay quiet, Garet watched the low-hanging stars, planning for Laura's return, vowing to make the H-Cross safe for her. As dawn began to light the eastern sky, his eyes closed at last.

Six weeks passed, and Laura remained in the dim room. She felt safe behind the thick adobe walls. When twilight turned to dawn, she opened the heavy curtains that covered the single window, but she kept the door barred.

Garet had returned every week, speaking to her through the door, but he had not asked her to come home. At first she was grateful that he respected her wishes. She couldn't face him, feeling so ruined, so soiled. The scars on her cheeks had shed their scabs, leaving angry red flesh, but the deeper scars, the ones on her soul, might never heal. She knew now that the perfect love she had shared with Garet was gone. And she thought that perhaps he'd never want her again. A rap sounded.

'Laura. Are you awake?' The thick oak of the door muffled Rita's voice. 'Breakfast is ready. Will you join us?' Rita repeated the same invitation every morning. Laura gave her usual answer.

'I'd rather not, Rita, please.'

'Then I will bring you something, *amiga.*'

A few minutes later Rita again rapped and, when Laura unbarred the door, entered with a tray of eggs and *frijoles* sprinkled with white goat-cheese.

'I brought enough for two. May I?'

'Please do.' Laura returned Rita's smile, but felt a momentary surge of nausea at the aroma of refried beans and fried eggs.

Rita put the tray on the sideboard, set two places on the small table, and poured goats' milk into two pottery cups.

Laura sat across from Rita but could not summon her appetite. She picked at the food, stirring it around the plate but eating little.

'What's wrong, Laura?' Rita paused.

41

'You take such good care of me, Rita. You . . . you .. .' Tears sprang to Laura's eyes. 'I've been here for weeks, yet you never lose patience. I eat your food and sleep in your bed and stay all day in this room and . . .'

'You are my friend, no? Would you not do the same for me? I think so. You are welcome here. For ever.' Rita reached across the table to grasp Laura's hand. 'Or until you feel ready to go home.'

'Oh, Rita,' Laura sobbed, 'what's wrong with me?'

Rita's face showed her concern. 'Are you not feeling well?'

'No. No, I'm not.' Laura had not menstruated since coming to the hacienda. She'd thought the shock of being so brutally assaulted was the reason, but suddenly she realized it was something else. 'Oh my God, she whispered. 'What am I going to do?'

'Rider coming.' Johnny sang out from the watch-out hill. Garet straightened from squaring a ponderosa log, adz in hand. Tom Morgan and Dan Travis worked in the sawyer pit, cutting pine planks.

'*Hola,* amigos,' Miguel Pilar said, reining in his palomino. His customary smile was missing. Miguel bent to scrutinize the criss-cross of horseshoe and boot-markings on the ground. When he raised his eyes again, he removed his sombrero. He pitched his voice low so only Garet could hear.

'It is not customary for the Pilars to seek help, *mi* amigo, but this time I must ask.'

It's not Laura! Garet felt as if a hundred-pound ox-bow had been lifted from his shoulders. His expression softened.

'Riders attacked our sheep camp at Ortega Lake,' Miguel said. 'They shot our herders and scattered the sheep.' Now Miguel's words came in a rush. 'We've always had trouble with the *Anglos,* even though our sheep were here long before their cattle came. But recently it seems to be more . . . what can I say . . . more people, more anger. Something more organized. Trying to drive us out. But we are not Mexican. We are American!' Miguel's voice rose with anger.

He searched Garet's face. 'My father asks your help, Garet Havelock. We must resist. My great-grandfather settled our grant more than one hundred years ago. We will not be driven away.' The palomino, feeling Miguel's emotion, sidled a few steps.

Johnny Havelock walked into the clearing, his rifle casually held in the crook of his left arm. He glanced at Garet.

'Miguel, meet my brother, Johnny.'

'*Buenos dias*, Johnny Havelock,' Miguel said. 'I have heard your name spoken among those who ride the outlaw trail.'

'I've been there.'

Miguel turned back to Garet. 'May I tell my father you will come?'

Garet nodded. 'We'll ride with you.' He picked up the adz and put it in the old wagon-box that served as storehouse for the moment. 'Tom, you and Johnny come with me. Dan, I'd be obliged if you'd keep an eye on things while we're gone.'

Travis nodded his assent.

In minutes, the four men left Silver Creek for Rancho Pilar at a lope.

The bell-tower of the old mission glowed gold in the waning sunlight as they rode down the hogback hill above Concho. Smoke from cooking-fires rose from the adobe houses. A glance at the quiet town told Garet nothing was amiss. His eyes continued their roving, scanning trees and shrubs, checking hill crests for movement, studying the sky behind them for tell-tale wisps of dust that said someone was on their back trail. Such habits die hard; Garet Havelock had acquired his over a decade of riding as a lawman.

The gate of the Pilar *rancho* loomed in the twilight.

'*Quién es?*' came a sharp question punctuated by the click of a rifle hammer.

'*Soy Miguel, con Señor Havelock y compadres,*' Miguel responded.

'*Adelante.*' The guard stayed out of sight.

Miguel opened the gate without dismounting, beckoning the others to follow. They spurred their mounts toward the hacienda. The tall thin form of Don Fernando stood in the shaft of light from the open back door as they dismounted. The sound of a woman keening came from inside.

'Miguel. My friends. I have bad news,' Don Fernando said. 'Pedro, a herder of our sheep, is dead. His wife mourns.' He led them into the kitchen where Paloma served coffee.

The continuing sound of keening pierced Garet to the bone. He bore Laura's suffering – and now another woman mourned because of violence. Anger boiled inside him. Would there never be peace for peace-loving people?

Garet hoped Laura could not hear the grief-stricken wailing. He picked up the thick pottery cup and sipped the strong, hot coffee, shutting out the conversation at the table. It was all he could do to keep from rushing down the hall to Laura's room, demanding that she let him in. Then he realized that Don Fernando was speaking to him.

'Señor Havelock?' The white-haired don's eyes, dark beneath his knitted brows, were filled with concern. 'Perhaps you are hungry?'

'I'm fine, thanks.' Garet forced his thoughts back to the problem at hand, trying to ignore the mournful sounds from the other room. 'Have you any idea who raided your flock?'

'Señor Havelock, we've always had trouble with *Anglos*. Many of them come from Texas where the chasm between our two peoples is very wide. The Pilars always prefer peace – with the Apaches before, with the *Anglos* and Mormons now. But we are not soft and we will not run like frightened lambs – sheepherders though we are.'

The don paused, focusing on each man in turn.

'Once settlers were few and the range was open and wide

enough for us all. Señor Buchard came. But we made peace – his cattle west of the divide, our cattle and sheep east. And we take our sheep higher into the mountains in summer, all the way to the Prieta Plateau. But now many others have come. Hashknife. Crossbow. Flying W. Crazy Eight. O Dart. The brands are many. Some on large herds, some on small.' He sighed. 'And every *Anglo* who makes his living with cows hates sheep, it seems.'

Garet nodded.

'It is strange to me,' the don said. 'We have raised cattle and sheep on the same land here for almost a century. It is simple. The sheep eat plants and shrubs but not grass, by choice, and cattle prefer to eat grass. If shrubs are taking over, graze more sheep. If there is a lot of grass, graze more cattle. The animals seem to have no problem with each other. Only their owners . . .'

'Don Fernando,' Garet said. 'First thing tomorrow, we'll take a look at where those jaspers hit your men. I've trailed more than one outside the law and Tom Morgan's eye is more than keen. Maybe we can figure something from the sign.'

'That flock was the first to come down the mountain this year,' Miguel said. 'The frosts have come to the high meadows. We can hold the sheep there for a while, but they must move down soon. The mountain aspens already show yellow leaves. Most of the sheep are still on the Prieta, where winter comes early.'

'If things aren't settled by time to move the sheep, we'll go along to ride shotgun,' Garet said.

'Our deepest gratitude, Señor Havelock,' Don Fernando said.

'Don Fernando,' Garet added. 'You have taken one of ours . . . my Laura . . . and treated her as if she were your own. We Havelocks owe you more than we can repay. The least we can do is help protect your stock and your people.'

Rita Pilar pushed open the door from the kitchen, bearing a platter of doughnuts.

'Laura told me you men are very fond of these. What did she say? Bear-tracks?'

Johnny Havelock laughed.

'You mean bear-sign.'

Rita favored him with a bright-eyed smile.

'Oh, yes. Bear-sign.' Her eyes held his for a long moment. 'Thank you . . .'

Johnny jumped to his feet.

'Johannes Havelock,' he blurted. 'Most folks call me Johnny.'

Garet grinned at his younger brother, who kept his eyes on Rita as he piled doughnuts on to his plate.

'You may have to make allowances for my little brother, Rita. His ma passed on when he was knee-high to a horny toad and he never learned manners.'

Rita flashed her dazzling smile.

'I don't mind,' she said, and disappeared into the kitchen.

Johnny looked dazed. But he dug into the doughnuts with the rest of them, and for the moment talk of sheep and violence waned.

'Don Fernando,' Garet said, wiping grains of sugar from the corners of his mouth. 'Miguel said two sheepherders were attacked. One's dead, but what about the other one? Any chance we could talk to him?'

'Ah, Antonio. The raiders' bullets hit him twice. One broke an arm and the other made a flesh wound in his thigh.'

'Doc Wolford coming?'

'My *segundo* went to ask that he come. But . . .'

'It's a ride from Show Low. Maybe we ought to talk to Antonio first, before the doc gets here.'

Don Fernando nodded.

'We can make the attempt.' He stood and led them through the large front room where Paloma sat with her arms

46

around the weeping widow. The men continued down the hall past Laura's door, where Garet paused, listening for a sound, a sign the Laura was all right within. He heard nothing, and hurried on to catch up with the others as they entered a large room at the end of the hall.

This room was the infirmary of the fort that was Rancho Pilar. Beds were built against two walls, and a cabinet with drawers and pigeon-holes stocked with medical supplies stood against the back wall. Near the door a wrinkled Indian woman sat cross-legged on the flagstone floor, grinding something in a stone mortar. In the center of the room the wounded herder lay on a waist-high wooden table beneath several coal-oil-lamps that hung from a rimless wagon wheel suspended from the ceiling. The flesh wound on his leg was bandaged, but his arm lay at an unnatural angle, despite its dressing.

Don Fernando went to stand beside the injured man, who peered at his patron with feverish eyes, murmuring something in Spanish.

'He's apologizing for not protecting the sheep,' Miguel explained.

'See if he can tell us what happened,' Garet said.

The don placed a gentle hand on the man's good shoulder and spoke. Miguel translated.

'Don Fernando says not to worry. He says that you are Señor Garet Havelock, famed lawman, who will see that Antonio's attackers are brought to justice. But first, Señor Havelock must know what happened. Don Fernando asks Antonio to tell us everything.'

The herder slowly turned his face toward Garet.

'*Muchas gracias*,' he said, and began his story. Miguel put it into English.

'The sheep they were settled down on the flat below Ortega Lake. We had brought them about fifteen miles down from behind Ecks Mountain. We felt good because two more days would put the sheep on our winter range. Ortega's Lake has a small flat where several hundreds of sheep can lie, and the herder's wagon can sit on the high ground so the whole flock can be seen. The night was clear and crickets sang to us that the frost would soon be here. Everything was very peaceful.

'Suddenly our two dogs jumped up, the hair of their backs standing straight up. They faced the knoll behind the wagon, and growled. We had no weapons but a rifle in the wagon, to be used if wolves or a cougar were to try for one of the sheep. But before we could even get to the wagon for the gun the riders came. I think more than ten. They yelled like warriors and fired their pistols. It was not the first time *Americanos* came, but always, before, they fired into the air and scattered the sheep, or tipped over our wagon. But this time they fired not at the sky, but straight at us. With so many bullets flying, it is no wonder that we were soon lying in our own blood.'

The sheepherder paused, his eyes reflecting the horror of the incident, then continued. 'The *Americanos* rode through the camp, shooting at us and then the sheep. They did not turn around. They did not stop. When they were gone the wagon was tipped over and burning, but the wagon team remained hobbled. Only a few sheep were dead, but Pedro was hit bad. The bullet hole in his chest bubbled. And I could not use my left arm. I used blankets to cover Pedro from the cold and rode to the *rancho* for help.'

'That is all, *señor*,' Antonio said to Garet in English.

'You noticed nothing about the riders, then?'

'*Americanos* by their clothes, *señor*. But they rode dark horses and their bullets struck me before I could see more. I am sorry.'

Garet turned to the don.

'We'll ride at first light. Maybe the sheep camp can tell us more.'

Rita rapped on the door and peered into the room.

'The doctor is here, Father.'

48

Garet glanced at Tom Morgan, inclined his head toward the door, and the two of them left; the doctor would not need them.

The aroma of fresh coffee wafted through the corridor, and they could hear Rita's laughter as they neared the kitchen. Then came Johnny's voice, followed by more laughter from Rita.

'We'll bunk with the *vaqueros* in the bunkhouse,' Garet told Tom. 'Would you mind tossing my soogans on one of the bunks? I'll be out in a few minutes.'

'Sure thing. I'm ready to hit the hay.' Tom went toward the door.

Both Johnny and Rita started as Garet entered the kitchen. He grinned at their sudden shyness, but then his face went serious.

'Rita. How is my Laura?'

The merriment vanished from her face, too.

'Oh Garet. One day she seems happier, making recovery, the next she's despondent, dark and gloomy. I wish she could forget and begin to live again.'

Garet sighed with weary sadness.

'Rita, she's been through more than any woman should have to bear. It'll take time. We have to be patient.'

'I know, Garet,' Rita said. 'She will get better, I know she will.'

'Deep down inside she's a tough, strong woman,' he said. 'Some day that strength will show. Maybe when we least expect it. Now, if you two will excuse me, I'll go say goodnight to my wife.'

CHAPTER FIVE

Laura sobbed into her pillow after Garet left. She had wanted desperately to open the door when he rapped on it to bid her goodnight, but she still could not bear to have him see her in all the ugliness of a ruined woman. She could not bear to see the hurt in his eyes, the horror in his face when her scars reminded him of what he had lost. And worst of all, she couldn't tell him she was pregnant. That she carried the child of that . . . that monster.

Garet had long ago stopped asking her to open the barred door. He merely asked how she was, if there was anything he could do for her, if she was feeling all right. She could see him in her mind's eye as he stood outside her door, tall and dark with broad shoulders, thick chest, and a slim, rider's waist. She could see the twinkle in his dark eyes, his dear smile, and her hands longed to touch the beautiful blue-black of his hair.

Dear God, she prayed through her tears. Dear God. Help me. Give me strength. And, God, please watch over Garet. He's so alone.

A tap on the door, and Laura caught her breath. Who could it be in the middle of the night? She took a quick swipe at her teary face with the sleeve of her nightgown, then she found the box of lucifers on her bed table, struck one, and lit the candle.

'Laura?' It was Rita.

'What is it?' Laura went to the door.

'I know it's late, but I must talk to someone. May I come in?'

Laura slid the bar from the door.

'Thank you, Laura.' Rita's eyes sparkled in the lamplight and a smile played on her full lips.

Laura returned the smile.

'Please come in.'

'Laura,' Rita began as they seated themselves, 'tonight Johannes Havelock came with your Garet. What do you know of him, Laura? He's very handsome, and he seems a good man, though a little . . . what do you *Anglos* say . . . rough at the edges? He has a strong face. I could see reflections of your Garet in him.'

'Yes?'

'I don't know what has come over me. It is midnight and the house sleeps, but when I close my eyes the face of Johannes Havelock is there. Please tell me about him.'

Laura chuckled. 'He is a strong man, Rita, and loyal to his brother. When Garet had trouble with Vulture Gold, Johnny rode all the way from Galveston to help him. Garet says Johnny's the best man with a horse and a gun he's ever seen. And Johnny's not a man to break a trust. He is a good man, Rita.'

Impulsively, Rita hugged her friend.

'I'm so glad,' she said softly.

In the gray of the dawn Don Fernando saw the riders off. Miguel led, Garet and Johnny followed, and Tom on his mule brought up the rear. They rode at a canter with their backs to the rising sun. Miguel kept them at a canter-walk rhythm until they topped the rise that overlooked Ortega Lake and the flats stretching north from its shores.

'Pablo, take care of the horses, *por favor*. We will inspect the

51

area where the murder happened,' Miguel said to the sheep-herder.

Garet put a hand on Miguel's arm.

'I think we ought to sit here and have a cup of coffee while Tom Morgan looks around. If there's anything to see, Tom'll find it.'

Miguel nodded. 'As you suggest,' he said. He picked up the blackened and dented coffee-pot sitting at the edge of the fire and poured some of its contents into tin cups.

'Havelock, come look.' Tom Morgan stood atop the knoll back of the overturned wagon.

Garet joined Morgan on the far side of the hill. With the stump of his right hand the black man pointed to a spot where the ground was chopped up by the shod hoofs of at least a dozen horses.

'That's where they came together, huh?'

'That it is. But I thought you'd be interested in this horse.' Morgan squatted at the edge of the trampled ground. Several hoof-prints showed clearly. One of them, the left hind-foot of a big horse, toed inward. It was a distinctive track, one that Garet had seen before. He glanced at Morgan.

'Yep. That's Max Baker's horse, all right.'

'Max Baker.' Garet's brow furrowed. 'Johnny said to look out for that bunch. But why would Hashknife riders be raiding sheep camps?'

Morgan shrugged.

'At least we've got someone to look for,' Garet said as he led the way back to the fire.

'Johnny, Tom found the tracks of Max Baker's horse. What you know about those Texas cowboys?'

'Max Baker . . . Well, he tends to hurt people. He horse-whipped more than one nester when he rode for Whitlow's outfit down to Waco. He'll use a gun when pushed, but he prefers to punch it out. Understand he broke a man's back in a wrestling-match. Powerful man, Baker. One to keep at arm's length. I'd carry a Greener with both hammers cocked if I had to face that *hombre*.'

'When he came to Silver Creek, it seemed those other cowboys were following him,' Garet said.

'He's got force, that's for sure. He makes things happen.'

'Could be he's behind these raids then.'

'Could be.'

Garet turned to Miguel. 'I guess we'd better find Max Baker.'

Miguel nodded. 'I can understand that, *amigo*. But soon our sheep must come down off the Prieta. By October they should be spread from here to the springs north of Saint Johns. I think my father would prefer that we see the sheep safely to winter grounds. Baker will still be here when we finish. The sheep cannot wait. If an early storm catches them above Nutrioso, we'll lose too many.'

'Let's go back to the hacienda and talk with the don. Johnny, you nose around and see what you can find out about Max Baker. I'll go back to the *rancho* with Miguel. Then me and Tom will go up the mountain, if that's what the don wants. But you stay down here and watch Baker . . . and drop in to check on Dan Travis at the H-Cross once in a while. OK?'

Johnny Havelock's face showed he'd rather ride to the hacienda but he aquiesced.

'Fine, Garet,' he said. 'Wherever you need me. And I'll get word to Dan.'

'Obliged. Miguel, let's ride.' Garet knew it would be midnight before they reached the hacienda.

Later, the full moon lit the countryside with a cold blue light, and the junipers and malpais stood out black against the pale tone of the grama grass. The dark ribbon of wagon road wound up and down the cinder knolls that dominated the country.

When the riders rounded the hogback above the Pilar *rancho*, the buildings lay dark. A wall of malpais formed a black border round the hacienda, enclosing corrals and barns, pig-pens and chicken-coops, and the squat adobe cottages of the married *vaqueros*. Nothing moved. But a wisp of smoke rose from the kitchen chimney.

The three men walked their horses down the hill to the tall front gate. The name 'Pilar' branded into the plank high on the gateposts, was just visible when a guard challenged them, then let them pass as Miguel established their identities. When they reached the corrals behind the hacienda they could see a single light in the kitchen. A *vaquero* came to take Miguel's horse.

'*Hasta mañana*,' Miguel said as he turned toward the house.

'See you in the morning, Miguel.' Was Laura sleeping in there? Was she all right? He turned the lineback into the corral, picked up his bedroll and gun and headed for the long bunkhouse, quarters for the unmarried *vaqueros*. Tom Morgan followed.

Dawn found Garet with eyes wide open and his mind filled with thoughts of Laura. He had a vicious rapist to find, and here he was traipsing around the country looking for a bunch of *Anglos* who raided sheepherders. He vowed to make the culprit pay. But his vengeance must wait. Even the work on Laura's new home had to stop while he repaid some of his debt to the Pilars.

He threw the blankets off. Today he would ride back to Silver Creek. Tom could go on with Miguel. He'd catch up with them later. Splashing his face with cold water and lathering it with a bit of soap, Garet shaved the sparse whiskers from his cheeks and chin. The red rims of his eyes revealed he'd not slept. But he'd gone without sleep before.

The dun was saddled and Garet had put his Winchester in its scabbard when Rita Pilar called.

'Garet. Please come in for breakfast.'

Garet looped the horse's lead rope around a corral pole

and strode toward the hacienda. This morning his limp was noticeable.

'How is Laura?' he asked as he entered the kitchen.

'She doesn't sleep well at night,' Rita said, 'but she's sleeping now.'

Garet's spirits sagged.

'Sit here,' Rita said. 'I have eggs and chorizo for you this morning.' She smiled as she poured his coffee. 'Will Johannes not be in?'

Garet returned her smile, 'He's looking for one of the men who shot the sheepherders.'

Miguel came in. '*Buenos dias, amigo,*' he said.

' 'Morning, Miguel. Did you talk to Don Fernando?'

'Yes. It is as I thought. He wants us to get the sheep down off the mountain.'

'All right. But I need to go to Silver Creek first. You and Tom can start for the mountains. I'll meet you on the Prieta plateau. Just tell me where.'

Rita glanced out the window as Tom Morgan saddled his mule, stepped outside and called to him, inviting him to breakfast. He came in, took a place at the table, and picked up a fork.

'Tom, could you go with Miguel to Prieta? I'll be along directly.'

Morgan nodded, his mouth full of scrambled eggs and chorizo sausage.

Garet downed the remaining chorizo and gulped his steaming coffee. As he rose, he took Rita by the hand.

'Tell my wife I love her,' he said. 'And that I'll be back soon.'

'Of course, Garet.'

The dun had two quarts of oats and a good draught of Pilar well-water in his belly, so he kept to his tireless single-foot nearly all the way to Silver Creek. As Garet neared the H-Cross spread, he heard the sound of adz against wood. Someone was squaring logs. Coming closer, he thought he could hear the sound of the big rip-saw in the sawyer pit. Touching his spurs to the lineback's flanks, he galloped toward the building-site. He rode into the clearing to face two men with Winchesters, cocked and ready.

Garet reached for his Colt.

Dan Travis leaned on the adz, a grin on his face.

'Howdy, Havelock. S'matter? Don't recognize your own cousins? The blond one says he's Willem and the dark one's Wylan. Claim to be Havelocks and twins, though they don't look alike to me.'

'Well, I'll be damned. Uncle Cadby's twins.' Garet relaxed. 'What brings you two here?'

Blond Willem shrugged a huge pair of shoulders.

'We heard Garet Havelock and his missus was having trouble so we quit mining in Bisbee and traipsed up this way. Figured me and Wont – that's Wylan here – might be able to help some.'

Garet smiled. 'Will and Wont, eh? Good to have you.' He dismounted the dun and shook hands with the two young giants. Garet Havelock stood six feet in his socks, but the Havelock twins had him by nearly six inches. And while Garet was uncommonly strong in the arms and shoulders, they had muscles earned swinging sixteen-pound hammers in the mines.

Garet quickly filled them in on the situation.

'The Pilars have been almighty good to my Laura,' he said. 'It's only right that I help them find those raiders.'

'You do that, Cousin Garet,' said Wont. 'And don't you worry none about puttin' up Laura's house. You just tell us what you got in mind for it and we'll get on with it.'

Garet took Dan and the twins over the house-plot, stepping off the measurements and placing malpais rocks at the corners.

'It'll take a while to square the logs and cut the planks,'

Will said. 'But we'll get 'er done. You just get on with catching them badmen.'

'Obliged, cousin.'

The sunset was turning the cotton-ball clouds a glorious gold that made a man feel good to be in the high country. Supper was antelope and beans, eaten with baking-powder biscuits and washed down with coffee.

'You boys keep watch at night, just in case. Y'hear? I'll take the first watch tonight. Will, you get second turn and Wont, you're number three. You wake Dan up when it starts to get light.'

Nothing happened that night, and after his watch Garet slept until dawn. He took jerky and cold biscuits from the larder and found the lineback grazing along the stream. By the time Garet got him saddled the horse was more than ready to move.

Darkness tugged at Laura's heart. She knew a child grew within her. A child of evil. She had not told Rita, though. How could she?

'Dear God,' she whispered. 'What can I do? I'm ruined. I so wanted to have Garet's children, but now that can never be. Our happiness . . . our life . . . destroyed by that . . . that . . .' She could not find words to describe her abhorrence of the fiend who had attacked her. First the paralyzing fear. Then the repugnant filth of it.

Laura clutched her slightly swelling belly. The child she carried . . . created not from Garet's love but from filth and violence. What kind of child? A monster. Festering in my womb. Oh, God!

Desperately seeking escape, she moved toward the light of the single window set high in the wall, pulled a chair beneath it and stepped up. For the first time since she had come to the Pilar hacienda she looked outside.

Dust rose from the corrals as a *vaquero* worked with a young

57

horse. Chickens pecked in the yard. She could see pig-pens against the malpais wall. Somewhere an anvil rang as a blacksmith worked. The barn door opened and Rita stepped out, her apron full of eggs. Three young boys ran to the corral and clambered to the topmost rail, where they sat watching the *vaquero* and the colt.

Everyday life at the Pilar *rancho*. Laura's despair deepened. What a wonderful thing it would be to have an everyday life. But that's impossible for me now. Nothing will ever be everyday again.

Tears burned her eyes. If only I could just cease to exist. Garet's life would be so much easier if I were gone. Scanning the room, her gaze fell upon the rack of mule-deer antlers high on the wall – and the Winchester suspended there.

No, Laura thought. A gunshot would be too punishing for Rita – and for Garet. There had been enough blood already. There must be another way. And Laura Havelock began planning her death.

Garet draped the dun's reins over the hitching-rail at Becker's store.

'Hey, Garet! Good t'see ya.' Julius Becker called his greeting from within the store.

'Howdy Julius.' Garet dismounted and went inside. 'Got a couple of favors to ask.'

'Sure thing.'

'I'm going up on the mountain to ride shotgun on Pilar's sheep. I told my men they could come here for supplies, and I'd settle with you later. Is that all right.'

'That's no favor.' The lanky storekeeper grinned. 'That's business.'

'Well then, I'd like to add my own supplies to that bill.'

Becker's eyes crinkled. 'Now that's different. Don't know if I can trust an ex-lawman.'

Ignoring the jest, Garet handed Becker a list of supplies,

and Becker set about filling the order.

'By the way,' Becker said. 'Your brother Johnny came by yesterday.'

'Goin' where?'

'Round Valley.'

Garet gave Becker a sharp look.

'Did he say why?'

'Sounded like he knew people over there. Is he on the wrong side of the law?'

'No. But he's got no use for lawmen either.'

Becker handed Garet a gunny sack. 'Bacon. Flour. Coffee. Don't have peaches so I put in pears. Baking-powder. Salt. Beans. Hardtack. That it?'

'Obliged, Julius. If anybody's curious about me or there's anyone you figure ought to know, you tell them I'll not take kindly to scalawags shooting up either sheep or herders. The Pilars are my friends.'

Becker nodded.

Outside, Garet tied the sack of supplies to his saddle, mounted, waved a half-salute, then turned the dun's head toward the high Prieta plateau.

CHAPTER SIX

Laura ripped a pile of rags into long strips. She'd asked Rita for old clothes or bedding, worn beyond use, for rag-rugs. Rita brought Laura scissors, needles, and sturdy thread. Old rags were not plentiful in the hacienda, but Rita found enough for a small throw-rug. Laura thanked her profusely, saying it was more than enough. Enough for what she had planned.

Doggedly she ripped and ripped, her brow knitted in concentration. The scars on her cheeks were losing their redness, but the wound in her soul festered and grew along with the child in her womb.

Before she could braid the strips of cloth, she had to sew them together end to end, an interminable job that sometimes brought a pricked finger as she stitched in the light from the high window.

Rip and sew. Rip and sew. Soon she was ready to twist the cloth strips into long strands, then braid them into a three-strand rope. Ordinarily, the braid would have been coiled and sewn into a colorful rug. But Laura's braid would serve another purpose. Her decision had given her energy, and determination to carry out her plan. The Devil's seed grew in her belly. Soiled by its presence, she knew she could never again face her beloved Garet. Ever.

At last the braid was long enough. She'd use it to hang herself from the antler rack on the wall. That would take care of the unwanted child and release Garet from the burden of a wife who carried a kernel of filth in her womb.

That night, in the flickering light of the candle on the table, Laura waited until the hacienda was quiet. No one stirred, and she knew she would not be disturbed in her deadly task. Carefully, she lifted the oaken bar from the door to make it easier for the Pilars to find her body in the morning. She placed a chair beneath the antler rack, climbed up, and took down the Yellow Boy Winchester, which she leaned against the nearby wall.

Garet had shown her how to make a loop in the end of a lariat. Now she made a loop in the end of the cloth braid and slipped it over her head. She pulled her long red hair out from under the braid so it could tighten directly on her throat. This time, when she stepped up on to the chair, she tied the loose end of the braid to the base of the right-hand antler, using a clove-hitch and two half-hitches. It would hold.

She stood very still for a long time, renewing her resolve. She thought of the baby in her womb, but her feelings for it were very different from what she had always imagined she would feel for her first child. She felt only horror, ugliness, and shame. What she was about to do would spare both Garet and the child much suffering. With her death, the slate would be wiped clean.

Carefully she adjusted the noose, so it would tighten and kill her quickly. She had read about such things. Then, her hands clasped behind her back, she kicked the chair from under her.

Her sudden weight pulled the braid tight as she dropped, her feet a few inches above the floor. Her vision blurred red. Instinctively she grabbed for the rope. But she could not get a hold on the braid to undo what she had done. As she lost consciousness, she thought she felt her child move.

*

Garet let the tough dun set his own pace. It was a long climb from Round Valley up through the cut made by Bonita Creek to top out in the meadowland east of the Blues. As the faithful animal climbed, Garet's mind went to his ranch on Silver Creek.

Lots of folks had come into the country in just a few years. Would-be ranchers, like Garet, could settle on almost any available water. The old-timers like Buchard didn't like the influx, but when the government gave the railroad every other section for forty miles either side of the tracks, the days of free range were limited. Some sold out to the Mormons, but Buchard and the Pilars kept to their traditions. In fact, the Pilar grant from the government of Spain in 1786 was recognized by the territory of Arizona and the surveying district of New Mexico in 1867.

The Pilars owned the vast tract of land that constituted their winter range, but the newcomers felt that Pilar sheep were range defilers. Many newcomers were from Texas, where sheepherders were considered pariahs, and they figured that driving the Pilar flocks away would make the land theirs to use as they pleased.

'Some's always greedy,' Garet said aloud. The dun pricked a single ear, and Garet patted him on the neck. Favorite mount though he was, the horse had never been called anything but 'dun'. He didn't seem to mind.

The dun huffed a bit as he lunged up a creek bank. Garet swayed easily in the saddle, helping the horse make the climb by keeping his weight centered along its backbone. At the top, he reined up. The country steepened from there on, slanting up to the high flat meadows on the Prieta Plateau. The junipers had given way to blue spruce and ponderosas, and a stand of blackened jack-pines marked the path of an earlier lightning-set fire.

Moving across a meadow, Garet came upon a wide swath cut through the grass by iron-shod hoofs. While he didn't recognize any individual horses, he could tell there were more than a dozen riders. They'd gone across the meadow at a lope, headed toward Prieta.

Garet had a bad feeling about those tracks. If the moon was bright enough he could ride on after dark. He hoped he could make it in time.

He kneed the dun and it picked up the pace. Darkness fell long before he topped out in the valley they called the Boneyard. The sliver of the almost new moon provided little light, but the dun moved on smartly. About midnight the land flattened out, forming a long swale with Flattop Mountain to the east and the Blues to the west. Garet urged the horse faster, pushing him into a smooth, ground-eating canter that would carry them through the Boneyard in a couple of hours.

The horse hadn't yet worked up a lather when Garet heard the sound of distant gunfire. Was he too late? He touched his spurs to the dun's flanks, and the tough horse jumped into a gallop. The tree-line was no more than a mile away, but the gunfire, coming from further up the mountain, continued as Garet reached the trees. He gave the horse his head, reining only to keep him moving toward the sound of guns.

The firing stopped.

Garet pulled up to listen. Then came the bellow of Tom Morgan's Ballard .50. And silence. Then far-off bleating. Garet clucked the dun forward again.

Sound carried a great distance in the thin air of the mountains, so there was no telling how far away the sheep were. One mile? Two? Garet shucked the Winchester from its saddle scabbard, levered a cartridge into the chamber and rode forward with the gun across his saddle bows.

The bleating grew louder. He reined toward the sound, all senses alert. A hint of a south breeze blew across his face, bringing the blood and offal smell of a slaughterhouse.

Off to the left a shadow moved.

'Speak up right now,' Garet barked, cocking the Winchester.

63

'Morgan.'

'What's happened, Tom? They hit the sheep?'

'Yeah. Took the closest bunch and rimrocked 'em.'

Garet dismounted. His knee complained as he walked with Morgan toward the base of the high, black cliff, where volcanic rocks broken away from the north edge of the Prieta Plateau, formed a rocky pyre. A pile of woolly bodies lay among the rocks, and the smell of their blood permeated the air. A few sheep had clambered to their feet and stood bleating. Some, squealing pitifully, struggled to rise.

A horse moved among the dark trees.

'Sing out,' Garet ordered as both he and Tom raised their weapons.

'It is I, *amigo*. Miguel.' Miguel's palomino came from the shelter of the trees.

'Sorry I didn't make it in time,' Garet said.

'I do not understand this, Garet. Why kill the sheep? They are dumb and witless but they hurt no one.'

'Because they are yours, Miguel. If you lose enough woollies and enough men, you'll have to leave this country. Then the whole Pilar land grant will be theirs.'

Garet shoved his Winchester back in its scabbard, pulled a handful of .44-40 shells from his saddle-bags, and put the shells in his vest pocket.

'Come on. We've got a job to do.' He moved into the pile of dead and dying sheep, Morgan close behind. Miguel joined them as they pulled the bodies free. Once in a while Garet would use his .44 to put a critter out of its misery. As they separated the sheep, they cut the throats of the dead to let the carcasses bleed.

'I was thinking,' Garet said. 'Sometimes the beef ration at White River is mighty slim, and when there's not enough game to be found Apache youngsters go hungry. Miguel, would you mind if Tom sent up a smoke? Hate to see meat and hides go to waste. What do you think?'

'We cannot carry the sheep with us. I count one hundred and twenty-seven dead. If the Apaches want them, the Pilars are happy to let them go.'

'Tom, it'll soon be light. Could you make a smoke? Tell the Apaches there's food here.'

Without a word, the black man faded into the trees.

'How do we get up on to the plateau?' Garet asked.

'Follow me, *amigo*.'

'What about them?' Garet indicated the sheep that had survived the fall.

'The first flock will move down the mountain about four hundred meters from here. When they pass, the herders will have the dogs bring these along.'

The men washed the sheep-blood off their hands and faces in the small waterfall that fell in a thin spindly plume from the top of the black cliff. Miguel swung up on his palomino.

'Come, let us return to the flocks.'

Once the horses had carried them up on the plateau Garet could sympathize with some cowmen's objection to sheep. As far as the eye could see woollies were everywhere.

Miguel noticed Garet's look of surprise.

'Nearly ten thousand,' he said with a touch of pride in his voice. 'One ram for every fifty ewes. And each year we have three lambs for every four or five ewes in the flocks.'

'*Patrón! Patrón!*' A sheepherder came running through the grass, pointing to the east. '*El señales.*'

A thin column of smoke rose from the high ground above the swale. Then it broke. A signal.

The Apaches arrived at midday. Morgan led them to the slaughtered sheep, while Garet and Miguel stayed at the camp, sipping coffee as pungent as acid.

'Miguel, there's no way the three of us can protect ten thousand sheep by ourselves,' Garet said. 'They'll be spread from here through the Boneyard all the way to the slot once you start moving them. That outlaw bunch could hit any where at anytime.'

'This is true, *amigo*, but what else can we do?'

'Where are your fighting men?'

'Pilar *vaqueros*, the men who care for our horses and cattle, are skilled at riding and with weapons, both blades and firearms. It has always been so.'

'Then why are they not here?' Garet asked.

'We did not expect this kind of thing. My father hoped your reputation would keep raiders away.'

'If we need those *vaqueros*, how many can we get?'

Miguel frowned. 'Without leaving the hacienda unprotected . . . perhaps ten, maybe fifteen.'

'I think we've had our warning. So better not move the sheep yet. Keep them here as long as you can. If they don't move downhill I don't think there'll be another raid right now.'

Miguel nodded.

Garet continued: 'I'll ask Tom to get the Apaches to keep white men away from the flocks up here in exchange for all that mutton. You ride for the hacienda and bring back as many *vaqueros* as you can. I'll ride after Max Baker.'

Miguel thought for a moment, then nodded.

'Your suggestion has the sound of logic.'

Garet rode down to where Tom and the Apaches were working on the dead sheep. He quickly outlined his plan to Tom, who went to confer briefly with a tallish, thick-set Apache who stood slightly apart from the rest, keeping watch. On returning, Tom reported:

'Alchesay says his warriors will watch. And I'll stay here with them.'

Within an hour Garet and Miguel were on the trail back down the mountain. They separated at Bonita Creek, Miguel striking a beeline for the Pilar hacienda and Garet setting out to track Max Baker to the ground.

'Laura. Oh, Laura. Laura.'

Laura heard the panic in Rita's voice. She felt comforting arms around her, then the soft fabric of her friend's blouse against her cheek. Then she recalled her own panic at the pain of the noose she had hoped would end her problems. A wave of soul-wrenching despair surged through her.

'Laura.' Rita smoothed her hand over Laura's forehead. Tears leaked from Laura's eyes, but still she did not open them, to look at Rita. Not after she had failed so miserably, failed even to put an end to it all. A tiny moan escaped her lips.

Rita cradled her friend closer, speaking in a low murmur.

'Oh Laura, *mi amiga*. When life is so difficult . . . when pain is so great . . .

'Laura. Please listen to me. Listen with your heart. I cannot put healing unguents on the terrible wound in your soul. I cannot bandage the gaping hole in your heart. All I can do is promise to always be your friend. I want to reach into your heart and pull out all the pain. That is what I wish . . . but I cannot.'

Rita's sincerity comforted Laura. Great sobs rose from the depths of her being, and she wept bitterly.

'Cry, my friend. Let the pain out. Cry.'

Laura clung to Rita until her sobs diminished.

'Oh, Rita,' she said at last. 'I . . . I can't bear it. I thought if I ceased to exist, then you and . . . and Garet . . . you could all go back to your normal lives. I'm sorry. I'm so sorry.'

'What is it, Laura? Tell me why you don't want to go on.'

Laura raised her head. A red line encircled her neck where the braided cloth had bitten into her skin before breaking under her weight. The rims of her eyes flamed red from tears, and her face distorted with grief. She could no longer carry it alone.

'Oh, Rita,' Laura sobbed. 'I . . . I'm pregnant.'

*

With a defense plan in action, Garet felt better riding down the mountain. He left word with Julius Becker for Johnny when he passed. He'd decided to exchange the tired dun at Silver Creek for his mousy grulla. Then he'd go to Holbrook, straight to the Hashknife headquarters. The men running the outfit ought to know where their cowboys were. And they'd be the ones to rein in Max Baker, if anyone could.

Garet reached the H-Cross at dusk. He spent the night with Dan, Will, and Wont, and noted with satisfaction two more ricks of new-sawn planks and a growing stack of squared logs.

Garet moved on early, putting the grulla into an easy lope. He'd not try to make Holbrook in a single day, but he didn't want to dawdle either.

He watered the grulla in Snowflake because there'd be little more until he hit the Little Colorado at Horsehead Crossing. North of Snowflake mounds of sandstone jutted from the sage-strewn land. Still, the horse was tough and his easy gait ate up the miles. Garet had plenty of time to think of Laura and the turns his life was taking.

A little over a year ago, he'd been trailing outlaw boss Barnabas Donovan, Laura's half-brother and mastermind of the robbery that had taken some $100,000 in Vulture gold when Garet had been marshal. The chase had ended in gunfire, leaving Donovan and his hired gun Juanito O'Rourke dead and Garet severely wounded. But the ordeal had brought him and Laura together, and he'd vowed to make a good life for her at Silver Creek.

In a year, he'd managed to recover from his wounds, get married, lose his wife, burn down his cabin, and leave his horses for someone else to train. He'd not found Laura's attacker. He didn't have a house built. And more sheep-camp attacks seemed imminent. But he knew Dan Travis would do a good job with those young horses.

'Garet Havelock, you'd better start pulling yourself together,' he mumbled.

He stopped the grulla on the high ground above the drop-off into Horsehead Crossing. Across the river, the black line of railroad tracks stretched east and west. Summer rains were long gone and the reddish-brown water in the Little Colorado flowed through a meandering channel in the wide riverbed. Garet nudged the grulla forward, and they splashed through water scarcely fetlock-deep.

Garet reined his horse toward Holbrook, a community of frame houses and whitewashed picket-fences that spread across the flats north of the tracks. He rode down main street to the livery stable, where an old-timer leaned against the wall on the two hindlegs of his chair.

'Howdy. Like to put my horse up for a while.'

The old duffer thumbed at the dark interior of the livery barn.

'Two bits for a stall. A dime for the corral. Oats is extry.'

Garet dismounted and led the grulla inside. The old man followed. 'You'll be Garet Havelock, then,' he said.

'I am.'

'We got us a tough marshal, Havelock. Stack's his name. Ward Stack. Maybe tough as you.'

'I'll go see him,' Garet said. 'Could you give my horse a quart of oats?'

'Extry, like I told you. I'll get 'em.'

Garet crossed the dusty street with long strides and hardly a limp. His rifle drooped from the crook of his left arm. Past the hotel, past the saloon, he stopped in front of the marshal's office. He rapped on the closed door.

'Yeah?' A young man with a deputy's star on his chest opened the door.

'Marshal Stack in?'

'Nope.'

'I'm Garet Havelock. I'd like to speak with the marshal when he's got time. I'm going over to Aunt Hattie's for a cup of coffee.'

'I'll tell him.'

'Obliged.'

Garet was on his second cup of Aunt Hattie's coal-black coffee when an intense young man of medium height walked in. He wore a star in a circle pinned to his leather vest. He stopped inside the door to survey the customers. His quick glance took in a rancher and his wife eating apple-pie, two railroad men, and a foursome of cowboys. Then Garet.

The marshal crossed the room to stand before Garet's table.

'Havelock?'

'I am.'

'Ward Stack.'

'Pleased. Cup of coffee?'

'Wouldn't mind.'

Garet signaled to Aunt Hattie's young waitress.

'Marshal'd like a cup of your mud,' he said.

The marshal hooked a toe under a chair and moved it around to the side of the table where he could see the whole room. He sat straight-backed, his eyes flicking from Garet to the window to the door to the other people in the room and back to Garet.

Garet sipped his brew.

Stack, too, was silent.

The woman brought the marshal's coffee.

'You got law business with me, Havelock?' Stack stirred a large dollop of honey into his coffee.

'No. I just wanted you to know what I'm going to do.'

Stack's gaze flicked back to Garet.

'And?'

'Some rowdies attacked a sheep camp belonging to the Pilars of Concho a little over a week ago. Killed one herder and shot another up pretty bad. The sign said Max Baker was there. Then a bunch hit a flock up on the Prieta. Rimrocked more' n a hundred head.'

70

The marshal frowned, listening intently.

'The Pilars have done me more favors than I can count,' Garet continued, 'and I told the don that I'd try to help out. I'm here to talk to the Hashknife Outfit. Baker's their man, and I want him called off. I'm going in peaceful, but I won't back down. Thought you should know.'

'Baker runs with the Jacksons,' Stack said. 'Quint, the old man, and his sons. You go do your business. I'll keep an eye on the Jackson place down by the tracks.' Stack drained his cup of coffee and stood. 'You were a good lawman, Havelock. I know the stories. This country's trying to grow up, and we need more of your kind. Ever think of wearing a star?'

'I'm a horse-rancher, Marshal. I've had more than enough of being a lawman.' Garet stood and thrust out his hand. Stack took it.

'Holbrook's a lucky town, Stack, to have you as marshal. You need help, you call on me.'

A hint of a smile touched Stack's face. He nodded and strode from the room.

Garet left some coins on the table and picked up the Winchester. He couldn't put off facing the Hashknife outfit any longer.

CHAPTER SEVEN

The headquarters of the Hashknife outfit overlooked Holbrook from the mesa north of town, where the reddish-brown sandstone and clay sustained only thistles and sagebrush. Further east the land turned pink and red and yellow and gray in the area known as the Painted Desert.

Garet's grulla kicked up miniature dust devils as he plodded up the incline toward the top of the mesa. The main gate was open and Garet reined the grulla toward a large frame house. Instinctively, his right hand touched the butt of his Colt .44 where it rode high on his left hip. He had no idea what awaited him, but he was ready.

He walked the grulla up to the ranch house where four horses stood hipshot at the hitching-rail. A slim man in dark trousers and vest stepped out on to the porch. His hair was clipped short and pomaded, and bands encircled his sleeves just above the elbows.

'May I help you?' The man's voice carried a hint of command.

'Could be,' Garet answered. 'I'm looking for Frank Jones or E.J. Simpson.'

'I'm Earl Simpson. And Mr Jones is inside. What can we do for you?'

'I'm Garet Havelock. Mind if I come in? I'd like both of you to hear what I've got to say.'

'Not at all. Come inside.'

Garet dismounted, leaving the reins dangling to ground-tie the grulla. He followed Simpson into the dark interior of the Hashknife headquarters, where he removed his hat, holding it in his left hand as he stood just inside the door. The big room was sparsely furnished. A large rug covered the floor, and a gun cabinet stood against the far wall. Garet recognized two Remington Creedmoors and a Borchardt Sharps. Someone liked competition shooting.

Simpson came back into the room with a pock-faced, woolly-sideburned man who towered over the slight Simpson.

'This is Frank Jones, our foreman,' Simpson said. 'Have a seat.'

'No, thanks. What I got to say, I'd just as soon say standing up. It won't take long.'

'All right. Say your piece.'

'Not long ago, four riders came by my place on Silver Creek. Said they were Hashknife cowboys. One was Max Baker.'

'Yes, Baker rides for us,' said Jones.

'Last week a bunch of riders hoorawed a sheep camp at Ortega Lake.'

'Happens all the time. Cowmen don't like woollies.' The foreman's voice was hard.

Garet had been speaking to Simpson, but now he faced Jones.

'Mr Jones, those rowdies killed one herder and sorely wounded another. Hoorawing a camp and scattering sheep is one thing. Killing unarmed folks is another.'

'Look here, Havelock,' Simpson's deep voice broke in. 'The Hashknife bought a lot of land from the railroad. Some of it is forty miles south of here. Part of Baker's job is to see that nesters don't settle on our land.'

'I reckon you and Mr Jones are new to Arizona,' Garet said.

'I hear Hashknife cowboys hail from Texas, and Texans don't get along with Mexicans. Here in Arizona, things are a bit different. For one thing, sheep've been here a lot longer than cattle. For another, the Pilar grant makes Don Fernando Pilar the largest landholder in Apache County, save the Hashknife.'

'I don't need a history lesson, Havelock,' Simpson said.

'You folks have been around going on three years,' Garet continued. 'The Pilars've been on their land for four generations. I reckon that puts them ahead of you. I also reckon it ain't part of Baker's job to kill unarmed sheepherders . . .' Garet looked from one man to the other. '. . . or is it?'

Simpson sputtered. 'No one's got orders to kill anyone. But if it takes a bit of roughing up to discourage squatters, then that's what it takes.'

'Mr Simpson. I suggest you think real hard about that. Be real careful who you rile when it comes to sheep and cattle. Else you'll start a blood feud that'll put Lincoln County to shame.'

'We can handle opposition.'

Garet turned to Jones again.

'Is that right, Mr Jones? You look like a man who's forked his share of broncos and tailed more than one herd on the Goodnight-Loving trail. Maybe you can impress on Mr Simpson here how bad war can be for business.'

'Fighters we can hire,' Simpson said. 'Jones's men don't have to get involved.'

'Mr Simpson. Folks find out your riders are killing innocent sheepherders, they'll hit your innocent cowboys. Nothing wearing a Hashknife brand will be safe. Take my word on it.' Garet turned to Jones again. 'Like I said, Mr Jones. There ought to be some way you can talk sense to Mr Simpson. You don't want a feud with the Pilars. They're gentle people, but they've got pride. And once they start hunting Hashknife cowboys, it'll go hard on your riders.'

Simpson snorted.

'You might do well to hear what Havelock's saying, Earl,' Jones said quietly. 'Mex *vaqueros* are tough fighters all right, but Havelock's the one to watch. He downed Juanito O'Rourke and Buzz Donovan. Stories about Garet Havelock run from here to the Indian Nations.'

'So what?'

'I'll tell you what, Simpson,' Garet said. 'If you start a war, you'll have to fight the Pilars, and they're a tough bunch. But you'll have to fight the Havelocks too. I've been shot at, and I've done some shooting. But let me tell you this. You ask anyone on the outlaw trail about my brother Johnny Havelock and you'll hear things that make me look like a shirker. Right now, Johnny's looking for Max Baker.'

Footsteps sounded on the porch, and Max Baker walked in the door. Garet half-turned so he could see Baker along with the other men.

'This man came looking for you, Baker,' Simpson said.

'Well, he found me.'

'Said you and some boys hoorawed a sheep camp . . . where was it?'

'Ortega Lake,' Garet said.

'We did.'

'One of the herders is dead, Baker, and the other hurt bad.'

Baker shrugged.

Garet got to the point.

'Understand you like to pick on unarmed men, Baker?'

Baker's neck colored, but he said nothing.

'What call you got to say that, Havelock?' Jones countered.

'Mr Jones, I don't know how well you know Max Baker. But my brother Johnny knows him from Texas. And he says Baker horsewhips farmers for amusement. Fancies himself a fighter, too.'

A growl came from Baker and he clenched his fists.

'How 'bout it, tough man?' Garet, turning to face Baker,

slowly unbuckled his gunbelt and laid the Colt on the table. 'There, I'm not armed. And I got a bum leg. Maybe you'd enjoy beating on me.'

'You're pushing me mighty hard, Havelock. But this is headquarters. Besides, I ain't got nothing against you except for your big mouth.'

'Look at me, Baker. Look real good. And anytime you decide to raid Pilar sheep, just remember my face. Because I'll come after you, I'll beat you, and I'll turn you over to the law. Count on it, Baker.'

Without taking his eyes from Baker's, Garet buckled his gunbelt back on. Then he stepped toe-to-toe with Max Baker. 'Remember this, Baker,' he said quietly. 'One small raid on Pilar sheep and I'm coming after you. Got it?'

Baker stared at Garet's cold black eyes for a long moment before he stepped out of the way.

'Ain't never been a man lick me in a knock-down drag-out, Havelock. But you're welcome to try.'

Garet spoke to Simpson. 'Simpson, you keep your bully-boys away from Pilar sheep, or you'll have war. No one makes money from war except them that sell guns and cartridges.'

Garet stepped outside and mounted the grulla. Deciding he needed another talk with Ward Stack, Garet turned the horse down the hill toward Holbrook.

Laura's neck still bore the bruises caused by the cloth braid. Her heart still ached, and her uncertainty remained. But she felt better having shared her secret with Rita. She began to think there might be a way to go on living. Feeling. Maybe loving.

The despair lessened further as she felt tiny twitches in her womb, movements of the growing child. Her child. To her surprise, she was beginning to think of that tiny spark of life as . . . her child. But still she confined herself to the fortress of her room.

In the sunlight pouring through the high window, Laura worked diligently with her braided cloth and crochet hook. Regretting her rash attempt to escape her misery, she coiled the long braid around and around, crocheting it with strong thread into a small rug. It seemed fitting that the Pilar household would wipe their shoes on the thing with which she'd tried to end her life. A tap came at the door.

'Laura, may we come in?'

'It's open.' She now left the door unbarred in the daytime, a major victory for her, though she still put the heavy bar in place at night. Rita stepped in. 'Padre Bautista is here, *mi amiga.*'

'Padre. Please come in,' Laura said.

He held both his hands out to her and she grasped them gently.

'My daughter. Are you well?'

'Better, Father. Not well, but better.'

Rita retreated down the hall.

'Come.' The padre carried a chair over into the sunlight. 'Let us sit in the warmth and light God provides.'

Laura joined him, sitting so that the sunbeams fell between them.

'Now, my child, I beg your forgiveness for not coming more often, but the lambs of my flock need me,' he said. 'But I am here, and God is here, too, for I come to you in his name, *mi hija.*'

Laura reached across the sunbeams to grasp the padre's hand. His kind, brown eyes held hers, and the warmth of his concern reached deep into her breast and released a portion of the guilt and self-recrimination she suffered.

'Father, I am pregnant.' Tears welled in her eyes.

'My dear child.' He looked at her with compassion. 'Do not cry.'

'But what am I to do, Father? I am a violated woman, and now I'm with child. How can I face my husband?'

Padre Bautista gazed at her in silence for a long moment, and when he spoke, it seemed he had changed the subject.

'Laura, my child,' he said, 'you came into this world through no effort of your own. It was your father and your mother and God who gave you life. Life is a gift . . . a precious gift. And we should treat it as such.'

Laura bowed her head, not wanting to look at him.

'This is what I think, my child. God gave you life. You did not have the right to try to forfeit it. Taking one's own life is a most grievous sin,' he said sternly. 'And it is made even more grievous because in committing that sin you remove all possibility for penance and forgiveness in this life. Do you understand?'

Laura nodded.

'In this life we sin and ask forgiveness and vow not to sin again and step by step move closer to our God.'

Laura was silent.

'You will not attempt such a foolish thing again.'

Laura shook her head.

'Good.' Padre Bautista patted her hand. 'God promised to make our burdens light if we trust him.'

'How am I to do that, Padre? I can hardly bear them.'

The padre smiled. 'Prayer will help,' he said.

'The Pilars ain't the only ones with sheep trouble,' Ward Stack said after hearing Garet's story. 'The Daggs brothers over by the San Francisco Peaks have been raided, and Pete Sponseller drives his flocks up from the Gila Valley. He'll run into trouble too, he don't take care.'

Garet nodded. 'Can't believe that the Hashknife is behind all of it, though.'

'Well, anyhow, Holbrook's my town,' Stack said, 'and Hashknife men walk lightly here. I ain't heard about raids in your country, but I'll keep my ears open.'

'Obliged.' Garet extended a hand. Stack shook it with a firm grip.

Before starting the long ride back to White Mountain country, Garet stopped by Aunt Hattie's for another cup of coffee. When Max Baker walked in Garet put down his coffee-cup and dropped his hands to his lap.

Baker came and stood in front of Garet's table.

'A fight you want, a fight you'll get,' he growled. In a light-ning-quick move, he smashed the table into Garet, pinning him to the wall with the leverage of more than 220 pounds. Garet took the brunt of the table-edge with his forearms, protecting his rib-cage.

Baker reached over the table and grasped Garet's leather vest in his two hands. He heaved Garet out of his seat and sent him flying into the opposite wall. Then Baker's boot caught him in the side just above the scar left by Barnabas Donovan's bullet.

Garret gasped, the pain dimming his vision. Baker grabbed his hair and proceeded to drag him outside, where he sent him crashing through the hitching-rail into the street. When Garet tried to get to his feet, Baker kicked him down again. Then he dropped to his knees astraddle Garet, his shins pinning Garet's biceps against the ground. He smashed his fists into Garet's face. Right. Left. Right. Garet's vision turned bloody. Blood clotted in his broken nose, forcing him to breathe through his mouth. He gasped. Baker laughed.

'You ain't so tough, Havelock.' Again his fist smashed Garet's face. And again.

Garet's eyes puffed and the inside of his mouth tasted like raw meat. He lay limp, going with Baker's blows rather than resisting, trying to lessen the impact. The world dimmed.

Then he heard a thunk and Baker's weight no longer pinned him to the dusty street.

'Can you get up, Garet?' It was Johnny's voice. Garet peered through the puffy slits of his eyes, trying to focus on his brother's face. He struggled to his hands and knees, then to his feet. He doubled his fists and, swaying like a wounded bull, peered around for Max Baker.

But Max Baker lay in the dusty street, buffaloed by the barrel of Johnny Havelock's Colt.

Marshal Stack came striding down the boardwalk with a double-barreled 12-gauge in the crook of his arm. He stopped short when he saw Garet's face. His glance took in the sprawled Baker and Johnny Havelock with his pistol in hand. Stack called to one of the boys in the crowd.

'Boy. You run and get Doc Heywood.'

'Yessir, marshal!' The youngster sprinted away, followed by three other boys.

Stack looked at Johnny. 'And you?'

'Johnny Havelock.'

'Related?'

'Brother.'

'Well, you can walk your brother over to my office. Doc Heywood'll be along. I'll get some of these gawkers to help me get Baker into a cell.'

Johnny nodded and pulled Garet's left arm over his shoulder. 'Come on, big brother. Let's walk.'

At the marshal's office Garet slumped into a chair, leaning forward so the drops of blood oozing from his nose would fall on the floor. His thoughts were beginning to clear. And he knew that he could not let Baker get away with this or the Pilars would never be safe. Somewhere, somehow, he'd have to even things up with Max Baker.

'Doc's coming.' The boy stood in the doorway, panting from the run. He looked wide-eyed at the battered Garet.

'Hey mister,' he said to Johnny. ' 'S that Garet Havelock?'

'Yep.'

'Jeez. He's the guy that shot Juanito O'Rourke. But he don't look so tough.'

Johnny chuckled. 'No, he don't. But take my word, he don't never give up.'

'Out of the way, son.' Doc Heywood swept into the office

80

with a bag in one hand and a roll of muslin in the other. He quickly examined Garet.

'Except for the broken nose, the rest is superficial,' he said. 'You'll look like death warmed over for a few days, but it'll pass.' He swabbed Garet's bruises and lacerations with boric-acid solution from his bag.

'Thanks,' Garet said. His split lip hurt when he tried to talk.

'Wanna look at Baker?' Stack asked the doctor. 'He's still out.'

'Be right there.' The doctor gathered his paraphernalia together and carried it into the cell. Marshal Stack, Johnny, and Garet followed.

Baker lay sprawled on a cell cot. Doc Heywood pushed the barred door open and set his bag down. He turned Baker's head to get a good look at the place where Johnny's pistol barrel had landed, then pulled a vial from the bag, removed its cork, and held it under Baker's nose. Baker strained to get away from the smelling salts. A groan came. His eyes flickered open.

'You feel sick, Mr Baker?'

'No, but my head is killing me.'

'Look here.' Heywood held a probe up in front of Baker. He moved it back and forth, watching how Baker's eyes followed the implement. 'This blurred or can you see it clear?'

'I can see it OK . . . but my damn head hurts.'

'Not surprising.' Heywood rummaged in his bag and came up with a bottle full of dark-brown liquid and a tin cup. He poured some in a cup, and filled it up with water from the *olla*. 'Here, drink this.'

The doctor turned to the three men standing at the barred cell wall.

'Marshal, Mr Baker ought to stay here until that willow-bark tea eases his pain.'

81

'I'll let him out in a day or two.'

'I'm getting out of here now,' Baker said.

'You'll leave when I open the door,' Stack replied, 'and not until.'

'Baker, you hit me some good licks,' Garet said. 'But don't expect it to be so easy next time. Somewhere down the line I'm gonna have to teach you some respect.'

Baker kept his eyes closed.

'Won't be no different next time, or any time.'

'One more thing, Baker,' Garet said. 'I meant what I said about the Pilar sheep. You been hired to keep Hashknife land clear of squatters. You go ahead and do that. They got no right to your land unless they buy it. But the Pilars are no squatters. You go after Pilar sheep and you'll get war.' Garet's speech suffered from Baker's punches, but his meaning was clear.

Baker turned his face to the wall and said nothing.

After a long moment of silence Garet shrugged and limped out of the cell block.

'That man considers himself tough,' Stack said.

'He is,' Garet replied. 'But now he's bit off a little too much.'

'Want me to stay here to keep an eye on him?' Johnny asked.

'No. Baker and the Hashknife outfit have been warned. Let's go back to Silver Creek, and you can ride on to Pilar's and report this to the don and Miguel.' Garet thrust a hand out to the marshal. 'Obliged to you, marshal.'

Stark grinned, a break in his normal stoniness.

'You ride easy, Havelock.'

CHAPTER EIGHT

During the weeks Laura had been with the Pilars she had not heard an unkind word. Rita constantly attempted to cheer her, or sat quietly to keep Laura company. She brought countless meals to the room, changed the bed-linens, and emptied the chamber-pot as well.

Guilty tears sprang to Laura's eyes. She had done nothing to deserve such kindness. And Padre Bautista helped Laura reach back to her roots, to remember the sweet psalms and warm spirit she'd felt as a child. How she'd loved the early morning walk to mass with her mother. How warm her mother's hand had been and how welcoming the spirit in the chapel.

A twitch, a tightening in her belly brought her thoughts leaping back to her real problem. The baby. A child of rape. An infant bred in the depths of evil. She sat up straight in the chair, clasping her hands over her rounded belly, her lips pressed into a firm line.

On one of his visits, Padre Bautista spoke softly.

'Let me tell you an ancient story, Laura. Perhaps it will help you see the child in your womb more clearly.'

Laura listened intently to the padre's kind words.

'Once in another land, far away and long ago, a young man fell in love. He worked with his hands and he had finished his apprenticeship. He was now a journeyman, old enough and

REVENGE AT WOLF MOUNTAIN

skilled enough to provide for a family. So he went to the parents of the woman he loved and asked them to allow him to marry her. Seeing a stalwart youth, a journeyman, a person who loved their daughter and would provide for her, the parents agreed to a betrothal, and it was announced. The young woman and the young man were very happy.

'Then one day the young man's world crumbled. His betrothed told him she was with child.

'What pain! What horror! What agony of spirit! Yet he loved her still. Tossing and turning in his bed, he slept fitfully, such was the depth of the burden on his heart. Then, in the dead of night, he dreamt of an angel. A being glorious as the noonday sun.

' "Listen to me." The angel's voice penetrated to the young man's very soul. "Hear the words of my mouth. I say to you that the child in the womb of your betrothed is of God. Think you no more of it, but marry her according to your vows." The young man knew when he awoke that his betrothed held life from God within her. And he respected her for it.

'When her time came, he was with her as the child was born. And they named him Jesus.'

Garet's face remained swollen and sore as he rode into Silver Creek with Johnny. His bruises had turned purple and the lacerations scabbed over. Black circles, now tinged with yellowish green, surrounded his eyes, and the white of the left eye was bright red.

Pausing in his work with the adz as Garet rode up, Will Havelock spoke for everyone.

'What's the other guy look like?'

'Hardly a scratch,' Garet muttered. 'Sore head where Johnny buffaloed him.' He dismounted and handed the grulla's reins to Dan Travis, who led the horse off toward the corrals. Johnny followed on his bay.

As the sun went down Wont Havelock dished out beef and

beans from a cast-iron dutch oven. Sourdough biscuits and scalding black coffee completed the meal. They ate in silence. Then Garet stood and took his plate over to the tub of creek-water that sat on the tailgate of the wagon, keeping his tin cup for another cup of coffee. The others followed suit, and they squatted on their heels around the fire, five tough men enjoying their coffee as the darkness deepened and the air turned chilly.

'Feels like a frost tonight,' Travis said. 'Better sleep with my slicker on the outside, I guess.'

'I see ice on the creek grass of a morning,' Will said.

'Johnny,' Garet managed to say. 'Miguel said the women at Pilars had made us sheepskin coats. Could you bring them when you come back?

'Max Baker did this to me,' Garet continued, his scarred mouth loosening and a hard tone creeping into his voice. 'But he'll pay for it.'

Max Baker was a tough and physical man, but Garet had seen nothing in him that suggested he had attacked Laura. While a coarse man might raise his hand to his wife, few would think of attacking a woman, much less another man's wife. Someone with a grudge against Garet could be the attacker, but no one came to mind.

Garet wondered what Laura was doing. Had she ventured from the fortified room yet? Was her wounded heart healing? Would he ever be able just to hold her close?

'Baker the one hitting the Pilar sheep?' asked Wont.

'I think so, but he didn't come right out and say so,' Garet replied. 'I warned him – and I warned Hashknife headquarters – but I don't think warnings'll mean much.' He turned to his brother. 'Johnny, you suggest to Miguel and the don that they get the *vaqueros* up on the mountain, would you?'

'I'll do it. But don't you dilly-dally too long. We'll need you.'

'You want we should help?' Wont asked.

85

'Maybe. If I holler, you come a running and loaded for bear 'cause it'll be war.'

'You call, we'll be there.'

Garet took a last sip of coffee, then threw the dregs into the fire.

'Think I'll turn in,' he said, putting the cup in the dirty-dish tub. He spread his bedroll out in the open on the far side of the wagon. The beating Baker gave him had sapped his strength; he was asleep before the other men left the fire. But the shadowy figure in his dreams disappeared in a spout of flame as Garet awoke with the rising sun in his eyes.

The others were up, and the smell of coffee was enticing. Garet eased his aching body off the ground, shook out his boots, and pulled them on. His breath rose, a white cloud in the frosty morning air.

His knee not yet limber in the cold, Garet limped over to the coffee-pot and poured a cup of the hot brew. Sips and then gulps warmed him inside and out.

'Johnny leave?' he asked.

'He rode out afore dawn,' Travis said. 'Seemed right anxious to get over to Concho.'

Garet grinned as much as his face would let him.

After a breakfast of biscuits and bacon, Garet sat down on the tongue of the wagon and cleaned his Colt, then the Winchester.

'Thought you was sticking around,' Will said.

'Got one place to go. Won't take long.' Garet went to saddle the dun.

Will followed. 'Looking for trouble?'

'No. But it pays to be ready. My face should tell you that.' Garet mounted, wincing as his bum knee went up over the cantle. The frost still covered the ground and the lower limbs of the junipers where the sun didn't hit. Winter was coming fast.

The sun rose and warmed Garet, but the swelling in his broken nose kept him breathing through his mouth. The dun was feeling frisky in the cool of the morning, so Garet gave him his head and let him go. The lineback streaked across the flats with his tail aloft like a flag. When the horse started to labor and Garet reined him in, he pranced, chewing at the bit and tossing his head. Garet wished he felt half as good.

By midday the hills behind the Forty-Four headquarters had lost their blue tint and the junipers and piñons stood out from the grayish background of frost-burned grass. Smoke showed from behind the long finger of land jutting out on to the flats.

The smoke came from the kitchen chimney of the main house, and someone had a fire going in the bunkhouse. Judging from the horses in the corral behind the house, and those standing at the front hitching-rail, Buchard's riders were in. But Garet wasn't looking for a fight, and he rode in with his hands on the saddle horn.

Dick Blasingame stood on the porch, unarmed as far as Garet could see.

'How do, Havelock,' he said as Garet reined the dun in.

'Howdy, Blas. Got a new cook? You're heavier than last time I saw you.'

The foreman grinned.

'Got married,' he said. 'Wife cooks right good, among other things.'

'You're a lucky man, Blas. Darn lucky. Me, I been married for dang nigh half a year and haven't had but a handful of home-cooked dinners.' Garet had meant to banter, but Blasingame's face went dead serious.

'Heard about your troubles, Havelock.'

'Thanks, Blas. Mr Buchard here?'

'He is, Havelock. Climb down and come on in.'

Garet dismounted and drooped the dun's reins over the hitching-rail. He paused a moment, then unbuckled his gunbelt and hung it over the saddle horn.

Blasingame held the front door open. Loren Buchard sat with his feet stretched out toward a roaring fire.

'Garet Havelock. Looks like someone went hog wild with your face. Been putting your nose where it don't belong again?' The rancher's voice still held its full quota of gravel.

'Could be,' Garet said.

Buchard threw back his leonine head and laughed.

'What you up to, boy?'

Garet turned serious. 'I know you're a cowman, Mr Buchard, but I came to talk about sheep.'

Loren Buchard listened carefully as Garet outlined the situation.

'Seeing as how the Pilars were the first in this territory, after the Apaches, I'd say they've got the right to run their sheep on their own land. But now a man and a lot of sheep are dead, Mr Buchard.'

'I never had trouble with Pilar sheep, Havelock. My range and theirs don't overlap much. And Don Fernando's always been a good neighbor. Far as I know, no Forty-Four riders were in on them raids. Blas, you know of any?'

Blasingame hesitated slightly, then said: 'No sir.'

'I'm glad to know the Forty-Four's not involved,' Garet said. 'But if you have the ear of any who are, tell them that any move against the Pilar family will bring the Havelocks in too.'

'I'll do that, Garet – and I hope your missus is feeling better.'

'I thank you for that sentiment, Mr Buchard.'

'I'd say you was gonna get run outta the territory.' Rafe Buchard came through the door and walked over to the fireplace, where he eyed Garet defiantly. 'Anyone with a face like yours should think twice about making threats,' he said. 'From where I stand, you come out second best. But that makes sense, you being half-Cherokee and all. No Indian could ever stand up to white men.'

Loren Buchard opened his mouth as though he wanted to say something, then shut it. Garet gave Rafe a cold smile.

'Rafe, lots of people have made big mistakes by judging things from what they see.'

'I don't want no half-breed telling me what to see. I know one thing for sure – him with the most power is the one in the right.'

'You keep thinking that, Rafe, and you'll end up dead. You'd better stay away from the likes of Max Baker and take your cues from your pa.'

'Get outta here, Havelock. And don't show your half-breed face around the Forty-Four.'

'I'll be leaving, Rafe, but not because you said to. I reckon Loren Buchard still runs the Forty-Four, and till he tells me I'm not welcome I'll come visiting when it's needful. Now, Mr Buchard, Blas, I've had my say. I'll be riding, but I'll be back around if there's anything I figure you oughta know.'

'You come, Havelock, and welcome,' the older Bushard said, and Rafe Buchard stomped from the room. Blasingame followed Garet outside.

'You ride careful, Havelock.'

Garet nodded and turned the dun toward home. Young Buchard had sounded like he'd been with the raiders. But considering that run-in with Rafe and Johnny at Round Valley, there was no way Rafe could have been up on Prieta Plateau to rimrock those sheep. Just where did Rafe Buchard fit?

The sun was down and it was almost dark when Garet rode into the H-Cross.

'Put those firearms away, boys. It's only me.'

'If I hadn't seen that ruined face of yours, Havelock, you'd a been riding in here dead,' Wont teased.

Garet laughed. 'Good for you. May come the day when those not so friendly will be riding this way.'

'We'll stay ready, cousin.'

'You warm me some grub while I take care of the dun.'

His stomach full of beef and baked beans, Garet felt things were looking up. Quiet clear night. Smell of juniper and wood smoke on the air. If Laura were here and the Pilars' sheep problem settled, I couldn't ask for anything more. Except maybe a son.

As Garet lay with his head on his saddle gazing at the broad swath of the Milky Way he went back over the things his pa had instilled in his mind. A man should never break his word. He shouldn't tar folks for something they'd done before he learned the reasons why. A man just didn't take what wasn't his. A man worked for what he got. And the Good Book said he wasn't to wish for something someone else rightfully owned.

People often thought Garet Havelock was a cold man because he showed little of what he was thinking. But deep down there burned a fire. That fire burned brightest for Laura, but it also fed his loyalties. Tonight the fires were banked, and he could reflect upon the situation without passions getting in the way. He ran a hand gingerly across his battered face. The bruises were not as sore. And the cuts inside his mouth didn't bother him as much. When the time came to whip Max Baker, Garet would move first.

He wondered about Laura. Was she getting over her despondency? Had her hurts healed? Wasn't there something he could do for her?

He didn't know how long he'd be able to keep making his weekly trips to the Pilar ranch. Winter was coming and there was no house at H-Cross. Before long the snows would come and while it didn't get deep here on Silver Creek, the creek would freeze solid and holes would have to be cut in the ice so cattle and horses could water.

Will and Wont had been notching squared logs and would soon start stacking walls. Garet wondered what he could do to repay these cousins of his. Getting out from under his difficulties was the only answer he could think of, because that was

90

all he'd want if the situation were reversed.

A horse stomped in the corral, and shuffling sounds indicated the horses were unsettled. Dan Travis grabbed a Winchester from the wagon box and went out to have a look. When he didn't come back, Garet took his rifle and followed. He found Travis crouching by the corral fence, peering into the brush. The horses stood with their ears pricked.

'See anything?'

'Nope. Some kind of critter, I'd say.'

'You watch. I'll go.' Quietly levering a shell into the chamber, Garet walked into the darkness, stopping every few steps to listen. He'd nearly reached the brush line when he heard a scratching, swishing sound. He stopped short. The sound came again, a little to the left. Garet took a few steps in that direction and stopped. Then came a scratching sound like a whine but not quite. Then, stepping carefully around a juniper, Garet saw the dog. The big lean mongrel lay on its side, tongue lolling. A big swatch of brindle hide was gone from the dog's side.

'Dan. Over here.'

Travis came on the run. 'My God! What happened to him?'

'Looks like he's been roped and dragged.' Garet moved closer. The dog had one front leg tied choking tight up to his neck with a pigging string. While he could breathe, likely he couldn't swallow. The drag might not have killed him, but tied like that, he'd starve or die of thirst.

Garet pulled a clasp knife from his pocket and squatted down beside the stricken dog.

'Easy, boy. I'm gonna cut that string off your neck.' He slipped the blade next to the dog's neck and severed the pigging string with a sharp sliding jerk.

The brindle dog stumbled to its feet and limped off into the junipers. Just before it disappeared into the trees, it turned and looked over its shoulder at the man who had freed it.

'Take it easy, old man,' Garet said. He folded the knife against his thigh and put it back in his pocket. Back in camp, he stood the Winchester against one wheel of the wagon. Travis had put wood on the fire and the eastern skyline was showing a thin line of light. Garet hunkered down by the fire.

'Havelock.' Travis pointed toward the trees.

The dog had crawled under a juniper where it could see the camp, but when Garet looked its way, the mongrel backed out of sight.

'Whatcha got there, Dan?' Will asked as he and Wont stashed their bedrolls in the wagon.

'Looks like Havelock got himself a dog,' Travis said.

Garet picked up a slice of bacon and tossed it over near the juniper.

'Here he comes,' Travis said.

The dog poked its nose into sight. It inched forward until it could nip at the bacon and drag it back under the tree. In the shadows of the juniper the dog bolted the bacon, then was gone.

As bacon fried and biscuits baked in the dutch oven, the sound of a running horse came from upstream. Moments later Johnny Havelock rode his bay into the clearing and brought it to a stiff-legged, hopping stop.

'Garet,' Johnny said. 'Riders hit the Ortega Lake sheep again last night. They killed Pablo. And Garet, they cut off his head. We looked all over, but can't find it. Miguel's fit to be tied.'

CHAPTER NINE

Garet scowled. 'Can't find the head?'

'We looked all over,' Johnny said as he dismounted. 'Garet, there's something sick about this.'

'Better you come over to Concho with me,' Garet said. 'We need to talk things over, and you should be there. You get yourself something to eat. Dan, take Johnny's rig off the bay and put it on that sock-footed brown you've been working with. Time for that colt to get a good work-out anyway. That all right with you, Johnny?'

'If it's got hair, I can ride it.'

Garet saddled his grulla and Dan got the brown ready for Johnny. Within the hour the brothers had their mounts at a canter, eating away the miles to Concho and Rancho Pilar.

On the way Johnny told Garet what had happened. The raid had come at dawn, riders sweeping over the hill and hitting the camp while Pablo was making breakfast. A young boy with the flock was on the far side. He'd dropped behind a clump of sugarbush so the killers didn't notice him, but the boy was so shocked, Johnny said, that he made little sense.

Why would they behead Pablo? And why would anyone want to hide the head?

A sentry challenged Garet and Johnny at the main gate, and would not let them in until Don Fernando himself sent permission. He was standing at the door when they dismounted at the corral behind the hacienda.

'Welcome, my friends.' The don's face was stern and his eyes betrayed a sleepless night.

'Where's Miguel, Don Fernando?'

'He left early this morning with some *vaqueros*. He wanted to have a close look at the scene of the massacre at Ortega Lake. My men brought the headless body of poor Pablo in this morning. Padre Bautista said last rites, but I could not allow his wife and two sons to view the body.'

'These marauders are going to get tough, Don Fernando. Your people must be armed and ready to fight.'

'We have fought before,' the white-haired don said. 'Pilars will stand. I swear it.'

Don Fernando made no comment about Garet's face, though the bruises were red and green and purple and the lacerations had scabbed black. Garet wasn't ready, but now he had to face Max Baker.

'We'll go after Baker, Johnny. You can keep people off my back while I take him down a notch . . . if I can,' Garet said. 'Now by your leave, Don Fernando, I'll go talk to my wife.'

'Of course. You know the way.'

Johnny remained with the don while Garet strode down the hallway and rapped on the thick oak door of Laura's fortress.

'Laura, honey,' he called.

'I'm here, Garet,' she answered softly, and suddenly he had to see her, had to hold her and tell her everything would be all right, no matter what. He grasped the door-latch and put his weight against it. The door was barred.

He sagged. This was more than he could bear. He'd been patient. More than patient. But now he needed her. He needed his wife. He felt the urge to break down the door . . . just to hold her once before he had to put his life on the line.

'Honey, me and Johnny've got to ride again.'

'So soon? Please be careful, Garet. I . . . I love you. When you get back, maybe . . .' Garet heard soft sobs behind the oaken door.

'Yes. When I get back . . .' Garet stood in silence, with his palms flat against the door.

Rita and Johnny were seated at the table when Garet returned to the dining room. Rita glanced up, then gasped as she saw his battered face.

'*Dios mio*. What happened?'

'Argument.'

'Should I call the old *mujer*? She knows medicines well.'

'I'm fine, except for looks.'

'Ness was telling me . .'

'Ness?'

'Yes. His name is Johannes, correct? And Johnny sounds so . . . so, how do you say, *jovenil*, juvenile. So I call him "Ness". He has no objection.'

Johannes 'Ness' Havelock wore a grin as wide as the Little Colorado at Horsehead Crossing. Garet cast his eyes toward the ceiling.

'Ness, eh? Well, all right. Come on, Ness, let's saddle up. I've got a man to whip. We'll go back to Silver Creek, change horses and then hit every Hashknife line shack between there and Holbrook. Somewhere we'll get word of Max Baker's whereabouts.'

They were about to swing up when the sound of running horses interrupted them. Miguel and two *vaqueros* charged around the corner of the hacienda at full gallop. Foam flew from the mouths of their winded and lathered horses. The tired mounts slid to a stop inches from the corral rails, and Miguel leaped from the saddle.

'What kind of monsters are these?' He stomped toward them, enraged. 'What have we done to deserve to be treated lower than savages? Tell me that, Garet Havelock, lawman, tell me that!'

Only after his tirade did Miguel notice Garet's face. '*Madre*

95

de Dios. What happened to you?'

'I think I got hit by one of the men who killed Pablo,' Garet said.

Miguel searched Garet's face again.

'My friend. Do they hold this anger, this hate because we speak a different tongue? Is it because we dance to different tunes? Or because our eyes and hair tend to be black and our skins are darker?'

'Could be anything, Miguel, but I think it's because your family has been here so long and because of what your father and grandfather earned through work and courage and honesty. Now others would take that with violence and dishonesty.'

The newly named Ness Havelock spoke.

'How does the law around here deal with Mexicans?'

'We are Americans,' Miguel said hotly.

'You know what I mean.'

'When a Mexican does a crime, he is often hanged,' Miguel said.

'That's what I thought,' Ness continued. 'I think they're trying to bag two quail with one barrel of birdshot. Mutilating Pablo should make other herders scared to watch the flocks.'

Miguel nodded. 'It has.'

'And maybe make the Pilars so mad that they'll commit a crime. Then Sheriff Hubbell would ride in with a badge and a warrant, and those people might have Pilar land for the taking.'

Garet agreed. 'You're right. And, Miguel, that's why you've got to leave the action up to us. Now we've got a handicap, too, being half-Cherokee, but I was lawman for near ten years and Ness here has quite a reputation on the trail – even if he does have a new name.'

The Havelock brothers mounted and rode for Silver Creek. Arriving after sundown, Garet hailed the camp and

96

announced he was riding in with a friend called Ness.

'Come on and welcome,' called Will Havelock. 'Hey. That's Johnny. Who you calling "Ness"?'

Garet told the story. 'And when a pretty woman gives you a new name, you latch on to it. Right, er . . . Ness?'

After the horses were cared for the men hunkered down to fill their bellies with hot food and coffee. Garet told the others about Pablo and the Pilar situation.

'Now you folks keep a sharp eye out. Me and Ness are in this neck-deep. Those riders may sashay over here to give Havelocks some grief. You be real suspicious of riders, single or in bunches.'

'We'll be ready,' Dan Travis said. Then, as if to focus on something brighter: 'We started stacking walls today, Havelock. You'll want to take a look come morning.'

'There's a good moon. Let's do it now.' Garet thrust his utensils in the dirty-dish tub by the fire. Will, Wont, and Ness tagged along. When they reached the high ground, Garet saw a flagstone walkway leading to where the front door would open. Malpais had been busted with a sledge-hammer and mortared into a two-foot-wide foundation. Big, squared Ponderosa logs were laid all around the foundation, resting in a layer of mortar.

'There'll be a shim between the logs right here.' Will pointed to a groove in the top of the logs. 'That'll keep the wind out. And we'll line the inside with planks. Wont's got himself a jack-plane and a good set of blades, so your missus'll have a fine house.'

Garet felt a lump rise in his throat. He cleared it noisily.

'Damn trail dust,' he said gruffly. 'Thanks, boys. I owe you.'

'Come on, lazy,' Ness called from his perch on the wagon tongue. 'We ain't got all day.'

Garet awoke with a start. Though the sun had not yet cleared the horizon, the smell of coffee and frying bacon

97

REVENGE AT WOLF MOUNTAIN

wafted through the camp. He hurriedly pulled on his Levis and shirt, shook out his boots, and stamped his feet into them.

'Your friend's still hanging around, Havelock,' Travis said, pointing at the big brindle dog crouched beneath a low-hanging juniper nearby. Garet took a piece of bacon, walked over, and dropped it close to the tree, then returned to the fire to take up his plate of bacon, biscuits, and gravy. The dog crawled to where he could snap up the bacon and retreated with it to the shadows.

Weapons cleaned and oiled, trail grub and bedrolls ready, the brothers caught the dun and the bay, saddled up, and mounted. Garet put the dun into an easy lope which Ness's bay followed.

A wisp of smoke rose from the pipe chimney of the line shack above Dry Lake as they rode up. The cowboy sitting on the south side stood as Garet and Ness rode into sight. They stopped some distance away.

'Hello the house. We're looking for Max Baker.'

'Baker's not here. He don't ride the line.'

Garet kneed the dun in closer. 'Thought maybe you'd know his whereabouts.'

'Mister, you look like you tangled with Baker.'

Garet laughed. 'You got it right, cowboy. He caught me off guard.'

'Tell you frankly, most of us don't cotton to that Texas crowd. Me, I'm from Montana. Horse fell on me a couple of days ago and I'm kinda letting m' leg heal up. Then I'll be riding the line and keeping my nose clean. But I heard Baker was headed for Pleasant Valley.'

'Obliged for the information. We'll mosey on down that way. Name's Havelock, by the way, and this here's my brother Ness.'

'Garet Havelock, the lawman?'

'Garet's right. But I'm horse-ranching now.'

'Heard about you from Tim Hunter. Said you're a man to ride the river with.'

'See ya around, Montana.' Garet turned the dun away. Marshal Stark had told Garet most of what was going on in Pleasant Valley. Now Garet mulled over Montana's information. 'Wonder if Baker's trying to organize ranchers in Pleasant Valley against sheep?'

'Can't see him as an organizer,' Ness said.

'Think we should drop by Zach Decker's on the way. He might have some information for us.' Garet nudged the dun into an easy canter.

The horses were fresh and Garet knew the way, so the brothers reached Decker's stone cabin while it was still light. As they walked their horses up the trail, they could hear the sound of an ax. Garet reined the dun to a stop when the woodpile came into view. A slight man with a walrus mustache was splitting chunks of juniper for stove wood. A holstered Colt lay within easy reach.

'Evening, Decker.'

The gunman looked up as if it was the first time he'd noticed them.

'Well, howdy, Havelock. What brings you down here?'

'Headed to Pleasant Valley. This here's my brother, Ness.'

'Will he be good Ness or bad Ness?' Decker cackled at his own joke.

'He'll be Johannes.'

'Howdy, Decker,' Ness said. 'I've heard stories about you. They say none can draw faster or shoot straighter.'

'Could be. You staying the night or riding on?' Decker asked.

'Riding on,' Garet repeated. 'I'm looking for Max Baker.' Garet told Decker about the Pilar problem. He ended with the beheading of Pablo. 'We heard Baker was in Pleasant Valley.'

'Don't take to Max Baker much,' Decker said. 'He's beat

99

on more'n one Mormon farmer. He's always civil with me, though. Came through here two days ago. Said he'd talk to Tom Graham and then go over to the Campbell spread on Cherry Creek. That's where you'd catch up with him, I imagine.'

'Much obliged,' Garet said, and the Havelocks rode toward the Campbell ranch.

CHAPTER TEN

Laura rose from her bath, dried and dressed. Again her glance went to the Winchester Yellow Boy on the rack of antlers, as it had countless times over the weeks. She stepped over and raised her hand to touch the smooth wooden stock. It bore scars, the kind that came from hard use, but the rifle looked no less deadly for them.

She carefully removed the rifle from the rack, its weight reassuring in her hands. As she tried the action, a .44-caliber shell popped out and clicked on the floor. She picked the cartridge up and reinserted it in the magazine. The rifle was completely loaded. On a hunch, she opened the drawers of the chest standing next to the antlers. The third drawer, waist high, held a box of fifty .44 rimfire cartridges.

She smiled. Now she was armed.

Gently she lowered the hammer and replaced the old rifle.

She went to the oak door and touched the latch. Then she pulled her hand away. Tomorrow, she thought. Tomorrow I'll open it.

Later, after Rita had brought the evening meal and they'd eaten, Laura sat alone again in the room with a candle for light. Once again she took down the Yellow Boy. Seated on her bed, she ejected all the cartridges from the gun, letting them fall on the coverlet.

In the flickering light, she examined each cartridge,

101

wiping it with a bit of cloth left over from braiding rugs. She got the box of bullets from the chest of drawers and wiped those, too, then replaced the extra shells and put the box away. She filled the magazine with fourteen cartridges and jacked one into the chamber, lowering the hammer before slipping the fifteenth shell into the magazine. She flipped the rifle to her shoulder and looked down the sights. She knew she'd hit whatever she aimed at.

Garet and Ness dropped off the rim into Cherry Creek country. The Campbell spread sat on high ground overlooking the creek.

'Let me do the talking at first,' Ness cautioned. 'If he's there, we'll know soon enough. And don't you get off that dun.'

Garet nodded and pulled his hat low over his face.

'Hello the house,' Ness called as they rode into the yard. The door opened to show a tall lanky man with a great hawk-bill of a nose. He held a Winchester casually in one hand.

'Howdy. I'm Ness, and this here's my brother. We heard Max Baker and Quint Jackson might be at your outfit . . . Mr Campbell?'

'Yeah. I'm Lige Campbell. Want to see Baker and Jackson, eh? What fer?'

'We heard there was some sheep talk and figured it might be interesting,' Ness said.

'Well, you're in luck. I think that's them coming up the west trail.'

The horses emerged from a stand of jack pines and approached at a walk. Ness nudged his bay over between Garet and the oncoming riders.

Jackson came first, then Baker.

When they topped out, Ness Havelock drew his gun. Campbell, who had been watching the oncoming riders, jumped at the sight of Ness's revolver.

102

'Sorry, Mr Campbell,' Ness said. 'Don't mean to be impolite, but my brother's got a private matter to settle with Max Baker, knock down and drag out.'

Campbell grinned. 'Always did like a good scrap.'

'What. . . ?' Quint Jackson kept his hands in plain sight.

'Beg your pardon, Mr Jackson. But my brother has something to settle with your riding partner, and I want to make sure things stay fair and even.'

'You. You're . . .' Baker sputtered.

'Johannes Havelock. People call me Ness. And this here's my brother Garet.'

Garet dismounted. He unbuckled his gunbelt and hung it on the saddle horn. He shrugged his shoulders. Still stiff, but he'd soon be warmed up. He turned to face Baker, who still wore a surprised look on his face.

'Baker, there's something I want you to think about. You had me down in the street there in Holbrook giving me the best licks you had and you couldn't put me out. I figure I took about as good as you could give. Now don't get me wrong. I'm glad Ness here happened along. But, when I get through beating you to a standstill, I've got some things to discuss with you.'

Max Baker threw back his head and roared with laughter.

'You? You're gonna fight me to a standstill?' He dismounted and hung his gunbelt on the saddle horn.

'Now, Mr Jackson, Mr Campbell. I'd appreciate it if you'd just back off and let these two settle their differences.' Ness kept his Colt in plain sight just in case. 'Mr Jackson, if you'd lead Baker's horse out of the way, I'll do the same with Havelock's.'

Garet and Baker faced each other in an open space about thirty feet across. Garet had worked with prize-fighters in Vulture City and knew he could win only if he kept out of Baker's reach. His damaged left knee would not allow him to dance around, but he could move quickly enough.

103

Baker grinned.

Garet crossed the space between them and rocked Baker's head back with a stiff right to the cheekbone. Before Baker could react and bring his hands up, Garet put his shoulder behind a left to Baker's midriff.

Baker aimed a punch at Garet, who was no longer there, and Baker turned to face the lighter man as he circled. Then Garet threw another right jab that smashed Baker's lips against his teeth. This time Baker's roundhouse right caught Garet a glancing blow that staggered him. But he still circled, keeping his weight on his good right leg most of the time.

When an opening came Garet filled it with a left, making a cut on Baker's cheekbone. Baker roared with frustration. He lunged at Garet, seeking to get his great arms in a back-breaking hold.

Garet pivoted out of the way, letting Baker slide by. He got in a rabbit punch to the kidney, and Baker went to his knees. Garet waited, his leg protesting, as the big man clambered to his feet.

'What say, Baker,' Garet taunted. 'You thought I was easy meat. Finding out different, eh?'

The enraged Baker rushed at Garet. A widespread arm caught Garet across the chest and both men crashed to the ground in a cloud of dust. Garet rolled away, avoiding Baker's powerful clutches, and made it to his feet. He met the rising Baker with a jab and a hook that rocked the big man's head back on his shoulders. Baker punched back. Garet ducked and grinned.

'You're a mighty strong man, Max Baker,' he said, taking another swing.

Baker staggered. 'You're no weakling yourself.'

Suddenly the two men were standing toe to toe, slugging it out, loving the contest, beyond hate and anger and even dislike. Two tough men in a contest of strength and stamina. Garet's face began to swell again. Baker's cheekbone leaked blood. And both men grinned as they flailed away, breath now coming in heaving gasps.

A huge right hand caught Garet in the side of the head and sent him sprawling. Baker waited for him, head down and rocking back and forth like a wounded bear. Garet struggled to his feet. He spread his legs wide and returned Baker's punch with one that started at the knees and smacked into the side of the big man's jaw. Baker went down. Garet stood spraddle-legged, chest heaving, waiting for Baker to rise. Slowly Baker came to his hands and knees, then struggled to his feet.

'Reckon this has gone far enough,' Ness said, nudging his horse between the two men. 'Ain't neither one of you gonna give up without you're dead.'

Garet winced as his split, puffed lips stretched into a grin.

'You're tough, Baker. And a better man than some would say, I think.'

Baker lowered his fists.

'You'll do, Havelock. You'll do.'

'Now. I think the proper thing would be for you two to shake hands,' Ness said.

Garet chuckled, and thrust his hand in Baker's direction. Baker grasped it and for a moment it was a battle of strength again. But Garet met Baker's iron grip with his own steel. Baker's face broke into a smile.

'Yep. You'll do, Havelock.'

'Now that's settled, we'd like to talk with you and Jackson,' Ness said.

'In a minute, Ness.' Garet slapped his dusty clothes. 'We need to wash up.'

'Right back of the house,' Campbell said. 'Ye gods, what a fight! I ain't seen so much fun for a month of Sundays. You all come on around here.' The lanky rancher led the way round the house to a barrel of water and a wash-basin. Garet and Baker rolled up their sleeves, grimaced at their skinned knuckles, and proceeded to wash up.

Refreshed, they came back to the front yard where Ness still held his pistol casually in his right hand.

'Max, Jackson, let me tell you a story.' Garet sat down on the front step and told them of the second raid on Ortega Lake and of Pablo's missing head.

'My God,' Baker murmured. 'Havelock, I'll put it to you straight. My job is to keep squatters off Hashknife land. I've hit a lot of men and hurt a few. But I ain't killed no one. Now. You're gonna say I was on the other raid at Ortega Lake. I was. Someone came up with the idea, and we was drinking some, and it sounded like fun at the time. I'm sorry that herder got kilt, but I'm thinking it was an accident. Now, I ain't been anywhere near Concho since I seen you in Holbrook. And you can bet Max Baker would never cut off a man's head.'

Garet gave him a searching look. Then nodded.

'All right, Max. But someone's pushing that bunch. Got any idea who?'

Baker shook his head.

'Mind telling me who was there?'

'Some I didn't know. Rollings from the R Connected. Walters of the Flying W. They were there. And that kid from the Forty-Four. What's his name?'

'Rafe Buchard?'

'Yeah. Him.'

'Anyone else?'

'There was a Frenchie. Don't know his name. And some riders from Alma, New Mexico. The rest . . . well, there was the Jackson boys and the Kid, but they've been here in Pleasant Valley.'

Garet made a mental note of the names Baker mentioned. He might have to go see them.

'Obliged, Max,' he said, thrusting his hand out to Baker again. 'I think you're a good man. But if I was you, I'd go easy with the horsewhip.' Garet lifted his gunbelt from the dun's saddle horn and cinched it on. 'Don't get caught between sheep and cattle, Max. People'll die, and one might be you.'

'Well, any time you wanna scrap, Havelock, you just come around,' Baker said.

'I don't want to trade punches with you ever again, Max Baker.' Garet laughed. 'Twice is twice too many. *Adios*.'

The heavy knock on Laura's door was forceful, masculine. Laura hurried to the door.

'Yes,' she said after some hesitation.

'*Perdon*, Señora Havelock,' Don Fernando said. 'Someone shoots at us from the south hills. We cannot strike a light without summoning a bullet. And I fear that tomorrow they will attack.'

Laura unbarred the door and swung it open.

'Rita will make sure you have water and food,' Don Fernando said, 'but we may have to ask you to allow us to defend ourselves from this fortress.'

'Of course,' she said.

'Thank you, *señora*.' The don turned and hurried back toward the front of the house.

Rita came with an *olla* of water, some bread, and a packet of the *machaca* dried beef. 'Our home was built to repel attackers,' Rita said. 'But of course the Apaches had no long-range rifles. Please stay in your room, no matter what happens.'

Laura slept little that night. Distant shots said the attackers were still there.

She shuddered to think that crude outlaws might soon be at her door. But surely the Pilar men, with guns and bullets, would defend her and the hacienda. Her hands trembled as she held them to the scars on her cheeks. Her heart raced. Men. Coarse, dangerous, diabolical men.

Laura woke with a start. Outside her high window dawn was breaking. Laura waited anxiously for any sign of attack, but the sun was high before she heard shots from the hill, then the cracks of responding rifles from within the *rancho*'s walls.

The firing came fast at first, then dropped to an occasional round fired by one side or the other.

Laura paced her room, stopping to listen each time shots were fired. The people who sheltered her were being attacked. The Pilars were in danger.

Dirty filthy murderers!

A new spate of firing erupted, more furious than before. The shots from outside the walls sounded closer.

Suddenly a tremendous explosion shook the hacienda, and debris rained on the roof. Laura knew she had to help. She grabbed the Yellow Boy Winchester from the antler rack, shoved the box of extra shells in the pocket of her apron, and lifted the oak bar from the door. With the Winchester cocked and ready, she ran down the hall to help her friends defend the hacienda.

Garet and Ness left Silver Creek for Rancho Pilar at first light. Suddenly, Garet held up his hand and both riders stopped to listen. On the easterly breeze came the distant sound of gunfire.

Garet spurred the grulla into a dead run, Ness's brown just a stride behind. Still, they'd gone no more than a mile when an explosion reached their ears. They could hear the gunfire, and they pounded onward as fast as the horses could go.

As Garet and Ness approached, they saw that the *rancho*'s front gate was closed, and armed men moved stealthily toward a breach in the southern wall. Black powder smoke hovered thick as the defenders kept up a steady fire.

Garet drew his pistol and fired three quick shots as he thundered toward the hacienda.

'Open that gate,' he roared.

Ness had his gun out, too, taking shots at the attackers. At the last moment, the gate swung open. Garet was off the grulla in an instant, taking but a moment to grab a box of .44 shells from his saddle-bag.

The breach in the wall was at the point closest to the hacienda. Pilar *vaqueros* fired from the roof of the bunkhouse. So far, the invaders had not come through the wall.

Garet and Ness took cover behind a mound of malpais. Unable to see the oncoming attackers, Garet shifted position, rolling behind a log that ran along the south side of the hacienda, his eyes and his rifle toward the breach in the wall. Outside the compound, he saw half a dozen men crouching, zigzagging, running.

'Here they come,' a woman shouted. Gunfire came from a broken window in the hacienda. Garet quickly squeezed off a round, and a man went down.

The *vaqueros* on the roof were at the wrong angle. The defenders in the house, plus Garet and Ness, would have to keep the onslaught at bay. There seemed to be two rifles firing from the house and three atop the bunkhouse. Where were Miguel and the *vaqueros*?

'Hold your fire,' Garet called out. 'They're gonna come in a rush. Ness, you take the left. You in the house take the right. I'll shoot down the middle. You on the bunkhouse can have what's left. Make your shots count.' While he talked, Garet shoved more shells into the magazine of his fifteen-shot Winchester. Then running men roared through the breach, stumbling over the rubble as they advanced. The defenders' rifles sounded and three men fell. Two dragged themselves outside the wall. One lay as he had fallen.

Another wave of outlaws surged through the opening in the wall. Rifles cracked. Men cried out. Powder smoke hung like a pall over the carnage. More shadows plunged through the gap only to be met by deadly rifle fire. Finally three quick shots sounded from the heights, and a cry of 'fall back' arose.

When the smoke cleared, four men lay inside the wall. One

tried to drag himself outside, one hand holding his stomach, the other scrabbling for a hold on the tumbled malpais.

Garet rushed to the wounded man. He grasped the front of Garet's shirt and pulled him down. His breath smelled of whiskey.

'Where do they keep the gold?' the man asked, blood bubbling from one side of his mouth. 'A whole room full . . ' His eyes clouded. He fell back, dead.

Garet loosened the man's death grip on his shirt one finger at a time, then stood in the gap, scanning the heights. The retreating men had gone over the summit; and he saw no further movement. In a moment, he knew why.

Miguel Pilar pounded down the road at a gallop, heading two dozen *vaqueros* riding double file. Garet stepped out to meet them as they rode in.

'We rode as hard as we could when the boy brought word of sniping,' Miguel said. '*Gracias a Dios* we're in time.' In moments, Miguel had men piling up malpais rocks to repair the wall.

As Garet stood looking at the dead men, a door slammed and running steps invaded his consciousness. He turned.

'Garet!' Laura launched herself at him and he enfolded her in his arms. 'I thought they'd killed you,' she mumbled into his shoulder. 'I was so worried, I could hardly see to shoot.'

'Shoot?' Garet held his wife at arm's length, savoring the pallid face, the freckles that stood out sharply against her white skin, the thin white scars that ran from high on her cheeks nearly to the corners of her mouth, the tear-filled blue eyes, the flaming red hair. His heart nearly burst with love for her. 'What do you mean, shoot?'

'Only Don Fernando, Paloma, and Rita were in the house. I heard shooting and there was a rifle in my room and you know I'm a good shot. I just grabbed the gun and some bullets and came to help. Then Don Fernando was wounded, so Rita and I defended the house because Paloma has never touched a gun and she was caring for Don Fernando so we decided to make those outlaws pay.' She paused, her eyes searching his healing bruises. 'Garet, what happened to your face?'

'Whoa. Whoa up there, lass. I'm fine. The don's wounded?'

'Yes, but he'll be all right. Oh, Garet. I was so afraid and so angry.'

'I don't know what got you out of that room, honey. But I thank God for it.'

'Oh, Garet.' Suddenly Laura was aware of her scars and her hands flew to her face to hide them.

'Laura,' Garet pulled her into his arms again. 'You've never looked more beautiful than you do right now. I'm going to spend the rest of my life just looking at you – and loving you.'

'Oh, Garet. I've been so foolish.'

'No, my love. And I'll see that nothing ever hurts you again.' They stood for a long moment in each other's arms, before Garet said, 'Now, let's go see about Don Fernando.'

They found the patriarch on a couch in the front room with one shoulder bandaged. His face was drawn, but he smiled as the Havelocks entered.

'Thanks to your brave wife, Señor Havelock, Rancho Pilar stood – as it has in the past.'

'Don Fernando. One of the men out there said something about a room full of gold before he died. I wonder why?'

The don shifted, looking for a more comfortable position for his injured arm.

'The Spanish explorers under Coronado and Ortega arrived in this country searching for the seven cities of gold. Then when those called mountain men came from the north and east in search of skins and pelts and what little gold they could pan from the sands of mountain streams, they found wealthy cities in Taos, Santa Fe, and other places across this land. Already my father's father had settled here and applied to the King of Spain for a grant of land where he could raise generations of Pilars, loyal to the crown. *Anglos* cannot imagine that Rancho Pilar was built by hard labor and sacrifice. So they like to think that my ancestors were *conquistadores*, that they discovered gold, and that that wealth is what makes Rancho Pilar what it is.' The long speech drained the don's strength and Paloma waved Garet away.

Laura clung to Garet's arm as he went outdoors again. Rita and Ness sat together on the veranda, while Miguel directed *vaqueros* carrying the bodies into the stable.

'Miguel, I'll ride for Sheriff Hubbell,' Garet said. 'I've got a hunch there are Wanted flyers on some of these men.'

'One man, shooting from the south heights, hit two of our *vaqueros*,' Miguel said. 'We will keep men up there to stop that happening again. It is a very long shot, and not with a buffalo gun.'

Garet remembered the target rifles he'd seen at Hashknife headquarters. They'd all been .45- or .50-caliber.

'Laura, I hate to leave you again,' Garet said, 'but Miguel and the *vaqueros* are here. You'll be safe.' He returned with Sheriff Hubbell the next day while the sun was still high. Hubbell looked over the corpses in the stable.

'I seen this jasper at a saloon in Saint Johns,' he said of one of the dead men. 'You're lucky, Don Fernando. If I were you I'd plant these four and fix that wall. No questions asked.'

After Hubbell left everyone gathered in the front room, where Paloma circled Don Fernando like a mother sparrow watching a fledgling.

'The nights get longer and the air is brisk,' Miguel said. 'We must bring the sheep down before the snows.'

'Now is the time,' Garet said. 'Looks like riff-raff around Round Valley's bought the tale of Pilar gold. I'll go see Gus Snyder and put a stop to those rumors. Honest ranchers won't attack a fortress like Rancho Pilar.'

Laura looked at him in alarm. 'Must you go again?'

'Just this one more thing, then we can be together.' Garet kissed her forehead. 'There's still plenty of daylight left so, Miguel, my suggestion is that you take Ness and Ramon and all the *vaqueros* except four to guard the *rancho*. Hightail it for the Prieta and have the Apaches ride shotgun for as far as Tom Morgan can entice them, and get those woollies off the mountain and on to Pilar land.

'Now if you folks will excuse us, I'd like to spend a few minutes with my wife before we leave.'

CHAPTER ELEVEN

In her room Laura melted into Garet's arms. Having him with her was heaven itself. He seemed oblivious of her scarred face and of the awful thing that had happened to her. His eyes told her he loved her, that he still thought her beautiful. And she wondered why she had been so afraid.

She loved this tall dark man; this hard, good man. And now he had to go again. But she knew she could do her part if the need came. No dirty filthy men would ever lay a hand on those she loved. Not while her rifle held even one cartridge.

Again he held her in a fierce embrace.

'Laura, I wish. . .'

'Oh, Garet.' Tears filled her eyes. Should she tell him? Could he feel her thickening waist through her dress and petticoats? How long could she endure without telling him? How long before he would guess? After all those dark and lonely nights of fear and self-loathing, she had the man she loved. She was content in his love for her. And they looked forward to their future on Silver Creek.

She cupped his face in her hands.

'There's something I have to tell you, my dearest.' She gathered her courage. 'Garet, I . . . I'm going to have a baby.'

A look of joy leapt into his eyes. Then came the dawning of realization. He stood stunned.

'My god, Laura! Why didn't you tell me? I mean . . .' He stared at her in disbelief as if seeing her for the first time.

Tears sprang to Laura's eyes.

'I'm sorry, Garet. I shouldn't have told you . . . just when you have to leave again.'

'There's never a right time for news like that, Laura.' He pulled away, and was gone.

Garet rode through the night. The joy he'd known, being with Laura again, had collapsed into a pile of misery. She was going to bear the child of a monster, and she seemed to want him to accept it.

A devil from hell had violated his wife . . . and impregnated her, leaving more than her scarred face to remind Garet of how he had failed her. He rode mechanically, his head bowed.

Gradually the rising sun burned the hoar-frost from the grama grass stalks, but the cold lingered in the shadows of the rocks. How Garet wanted to get his hands on that fiend. He'd make him pay for what he'd done. Had the Jicarilla found anything? No word meant only that the Indian was still looking.

Garet ground his teeth. What could he do?

He realized that he loved Laura now more than ever. Their long separation had brought home to him just how much she meant to him. But this. How much must a man bear?

Garet passed Becker's store with no more than a perfunctory wave at Julius. At least a dozen horses stood at the hitching-rail in front of the saloon at Round Valley, but Garet kneed the grulla toward Gus Snyder's stronghold.

'Hold up, Havelock.' A man stepped into the road in front of the grulla.

Garet reined in. 'I'd like to go on up to the house and speak to Mr Snyder.'

'Obliged to take your hardware,' the man said.

Garet handed his guns over.

The man walked ahead toward Gus Snyder's fortress house.

'Mr Havelock to see Mr Snyder,' the man roared when he

115

was fifty feet from the front door. As before, riflemen appeared, holding their weapons casually, but ready.

Gus Snyder himself opened the heavy front door.

'Welcome, Havelock. God! What happened to your face?'

'Me and Max Baker had a little disagreement, but we settled it. He'll not be hoorawing Pilar sheep any more. Er, Mr Snyder. . . .'

'Gus.'

'Right, Gus. Something has come up.'

'Well, come in, then.'

Garet dismounted and faltered at the steps when he took the first one with his left leg, but the brace held and he was able to make the step without falling.

'Knee bother you,' Snyder said.

'Some, when it gets cold.'

Snyder pushed the big door inward and ushered Garet into the dim parlor, motioning for him to have a seat. Snyder turned a chair around and sat astraddle with his arms on the back of the chair and his chin on his arms.

'My God, you look awful.' Snyder grinned. 'Like to have seen that scrap. Mighta been instructional.'

'Doubt it. It was all I could do to keep myself above water. Baker's one tough cowboy.'

'So what you got to tell me?'

Garet went through the whole story, including the rumor of gold.

'Now Gus, I don't think there's any hidden gold on Rancho Pilar. Admitted, I haven't seen every nook and cranny, but I'm inclined to think not.'

Snyder nodded, sucking at his lower lip.

'Sheriff Hubbell seemed to think some of the four men killed in the attack on the Pilars might hail from this neck of the woods. And I'm figuring it's talk of gold that got them heated up.'

The outlaw's eyes slimmed down a notch.

'I'd take it kindly if you and Jim over to the saloon could get it out that the gold at the Pilars is just rumor,' Garet said.

'That could be hard to do, Havelock. Ya see, there was a young feller in the saloon just the other day who said his own mama seen that gold. He said a few good men could take it all away and split it up. A story like that's hard to put down, Havelock.'

'Looks like I need to talk to Rafe Buchard.'

'Be a likely place to start.'

'You think about that rumor, Gus. Don't know what's on young Buchard's mind, but I'd bet my good name there's something other than gold.'

'You may be right, and I'll think on it. Now don't get me wrong. I'm not the kind that would ransack a man's home for gold. Taking a little from Bluecoats now and then . . . well, I figure them Yankees owe me.'

'Could you pass the word on to Jim?'

'I'll talk to him.' Snyder extended his hand with a small tight smile.

Garet shook hands, replaced his flat-crowned Stetson and pulled open the heavy door.

'Mr Havelock's leaving. Give him his hardware.'

Garet accepted his Colt and Winchester, put them in their accustomed places. He swung up on the grulla.

'Much obliged, Mr Snyder.'

'Ride careful, Havelock. That young Buchard's a close cousin to a rattler.'

Garet raised a finger to the brim of his hat and reined the grulla away. He passed the saloon without a glance, reaching into a saddle-bag for some hardtack to make a midday meal. With luck, he'd be at the Forty-Four before dark.

Rafe Buchard said his mother had seen the Pilar gold. But his mother's dead, and what would she have to do with the Pilars? Rafe's a Mexican hater. Hates anyone of another color. And him as dark as me. I'm half-Cherokee, so what does that make him? Half . . . Mexican?

Garet straightened in the saddle. Maybe Buchard's wife had been connected to the Pilars.

The grulla felt Garet's tension and picked up his pace, so there was still daylight left when Garet reined the horse up at the Forty-Four. Dick Blasingame came out of the bunkhouse.

'How's it going, Havelock? What can I do ya for?'

'Thought maybe I could talk to Mr Buchard and Rafe.'

'Both gone.'

'When do you expect Mr Buchard back?'

'Day after tomorrow sometime, I'd reckon. Why?'

'Blas, mind if I ask you something?'

The foreman shrugged. 'Shoot.'

'Is there any connection between Mr Buchard's wife and the Pilars?'

Blasingame scrubbed a toe in the dirt.

'I don't reckon it's a secret. Missus Buchard was Mexican. She and the boss got hitched way back in the sixties, right after the war. There wasn't nothing here then but El Vadito, Concho, and Valle Ronde. No white settlers. Just the Mexes and the Apaches.'

'What about Mr Buchard's wife?'

'Pretty as a sego lily, they say. But she had a mean streak in her and I think she might have been a little, well, unhinged.'

'What about the Pilars?'

'I'm not sure. But somehow the missus thought the Pilars had stole something from her family, 'cept far as I know she had no family.'

'Pilars are moving sheep down the mountain, Blas. The *vaqueros* are riding shotgun and Tom Morgan's along with a bunch of White Mountain Apaches. You might want to tell anyone who's been hoorawing Pilar sheep camps that now's not a good time.'

'You bet.'

'I'll be back, Blas, to speak with Mr Buchard.'

118

Garet reached the H-Cross camp just before midnight.

'Hey, Garet.' Dan Travis crawled out of his blankets, shivering, and put some wood on the fire to heat coffee.

'Much obliged, Dan. Don't know as I've had any real grub since yesterday.' After wolfing down bacon, beans, and cold sourdough biscuits, Garet relieved himself in the new two-hole outhouse Will and Wont had built back of the ranch house. The walls of the house were now nearly high enough to start laying rafters. Will had piled malpais for a forge where he made hinges and latches and the like for the new house. Garet felt a surge of pride in his cousins and the house they were building for his lady.

He shrugged deeper into his sheepskin coat. Damn. His breath jogged out white before him. Just into November and freezing cold at night. He pulled an extra blanket from the wagon to add to his bedroll. Using the saddle blanket as a ground-cloth, he rolled up in the blankets, pulled the tarp over the top, and dropped into a sound sleep.

After a quick breakfast he was on the dun, riding for Ortega Lake. He'd take a look at the sheep camp, though there might be nothing there. Tomorrow, he'd ride back to the Forty-Four.

The dun was cat-footing along the edge of the canyon south of the lake when a bullet knocked Garet from the saddle.

Happy to be helping around the house again, Laura often felt the child's movement now. What could she do to help Garet accept it? There was no doubt in her heart that he would, in time, in his own way; she refused to accept the possibility of rejection. But she often prayed: 'Dear God, whatever happens to me, I can endure, but please help these two to love each other. Please. Please.'

With the dishes dried and placed in their cabinets, Laura stood gazing out the window.

'Give me a pistol, Rita,' she said suddenly.

'A pistol? Why?'

'I want to go feed the chickens and gather the eggs, but I'm not ready to go outside without a weapon.'

Rita went to the gun-cabinet in the living-room and returned with a pearl-handled .41-caliber Colt Lightning.

Laura took the weapon, checked its loads, and put it in her pocket. Then she picked up the pan of table-leavings, and resolutely marched outside.

The wind buffeted her hair as she rounded the corner of the hacienda and she paused to take a deep breath. It was good to feel the freedom from fear, but her right hand kept a white-knuckled grip on the butt of the Lightning.

Chickens flocked from the four corners of the walled *rancho*, running for the potato-peelings, eggshells, and corn-cobs Laura flung in a wide swath across the bare ground.

Cautiously she entered the chicken coop. A row of bins against one wall served as nests. From them Laura gathered eleven eggs, placing them in the empty pan. She stayed clear of the broody hen on one of the nests.

'*Señora.*'

Laura whirled, drawing the pistol and pointing it into Ramon's face, her finger taking up the slack in the trigger.

'*Señora. Por favor.*' He held up his hands. 'I mean you no harm.'

'Ramon!' Laura lowered her pistol. 'I'm sorry. You surprised me.' She smiled. 'At least I didn't break any eggs. What is it?'

'*Señora.* Señor Havelock. He cannot be located.'

Panic rose in Laura's throat. Something terrible had happened. What would she do if Garet never came back? What if Garet was lying out there somewhere? Hurt, or dead?

'Sometimes there is nothing we can do but hope,' Rita told her as they sat together after the evening meal, '. . . and pray.'

Laura nodded. 'And where is Ness?'

Rita smiled. 'Ness is with Miguel and the *vaqueros* helping bring the sheep from Prieta. I think he is safe, as is Miguel. Is everything all right with you?'

'If I only I knew whether he was alive.' Laura fell silent.

Rita grasped her friend's hands.

'Hope, my friend. Hope.'

Garet was first aware of a snuffling at his hair. Then the searing pain hit him. He opened his eyes a crack and looked at the muzzle of the dun horse. He moved his head. Pain. He moved his left arm. Pain coursed up his back.

He tried to focus. He remembered getting knocked off the horse . . . by what? He inched his right hand across his chest and found a hole in his shirt.

He shivered with cold. It was daylight, but the canyon bottom remained in shadow. Where was his coat? He made a swipe with his right hand. Nothing. The dun snuffled his hair again.

God, he was weak. He explored the center of the pain in his head and found his hair matted with blood over an egg-sized knot.

Weak. Gotta move. So cold. He laid his right arm next to his body and tried to roll over on to his stomach. Something seemed to be holding him to the ground. Then it broke loose. Biting his lip against the pain in his shoulder and back, he rolled on to his right side. The ground where his left shoulder had been was soaked with blood. It had dried and stuck to his shirt and to the wound. Garet was no longer tied to the earth by his own blood, but the wound started bleeding again, and his movement made him dizzy and nauseous. He lowered his face to his arms, flinching at the pain when his cheek touched the sleeve of his shirt. His senses faded and his head drooped on to his folded arms.

It was dark when Garet regained consciousness. He was trembling, and his teeth chattered. He had to move. One at a time, he discovered his wounds. Had he been shot? And he must have taken a fall. Hit his head on the rocks. But where was his coat? His vest? His brace? His searching hand found a pile of sheepskin pieces. The stabbing pain told him not to move his left arm, so he used his right hand, stuffing the pieces of sheepskin inside his shirt, shoving them as far up his back and around his shoulders and sides as he could. It was a slow, painful task that exhausted him. A portion of one coat-sleeve remained relatively whole, and he pulled it on over his left arm.

He remembered seeing the dun when he'd first awakened. He whistled through his teeth. Then again louder. In a moment he heard the dun's footsteps and the squeak of saddle leather. The dun blew at his smell, then nudged him with his nose.

Garet tried raising his head, but the nausea attacked again and he could only grasp the dragging reins. He tugged, clucking at the horse until he moved around and faced downstream toward Ortega Lake.

Taking deep breaths, he tried to clear his head. Without his brace, he couldn't mount. He was too weak to walk. He edged around until he lay with the stirrup above his right hand. That put his wounded left side down, but the coat-sleeve might help. If he could keep that left arm clamped tight and take the bumps on it . . .

He reached up and hooked his right hand through the stirrup. The reins would have to drag. He clucked at the dun. It took a step. Then another. Garet gritted his teeth at the pain as his body bumped along the uneven ground. He lost the loose coat-sleeve.

Twenty paces down the trail he could no longer keep his grip. He whoaed the dun and rested. Maybe there was a better way. His head ached. His face stung. He touched his cheek. Cut. Slashed. His side and back began to bleed again. But if he didn't get out of this canyon, if he didn't move . . .

Garet hooked the stirrup with his right forearm this time, hanging by the crook of his elbow, which raised his left shoulder off the ground. Man and horse went nearly fifty yards before Garet had to halt.

The cold was seeping into his bones. He tried to concentrate, to focus. Move. Move. Move.

Time and again the patient horse started and stopped at Garet's commands. By the time the moon rose they had covered nearly a mile. The dun walked catty-corner, careful not to step on the man dragging from the stirrup, its breath making clouds of white in the still night air. Blades of browned grass and willows along the creek sparkled with frost. With the high moon now providing light, Garet and the horse were nearly to the place where the canyon's malpais walls dropped away and the stream meandered down to Ortega Lake.

Garet's fingers had lost their feeling but the sheepskin under his shirt helped save precious body heat. His wounds still leaked, and he held on to the stirrup more with will power than with physical strength.

When he couldn't hang on any longer he mustered his strength, pulled off his belt, rebuckled it, slipped it through the stirrup, then back through its loop, so it could not come off. He slipped his right wrist through the belt so the force of the dun pulling, tightening the loop around his hand, would keep it from slipping off. Then clucking to the dun, they moved off again, the horse dragging Garet one step at a time.

Sometime later Garet lost consciousness. But the dun kept moving, careful not to step on its burden. When it reached the edge of Ortega Lake, the horse stopped.

CHAPTER TWELVE

'Amen.'

'Amen?' Garet muttered, his eyes still closed. He lay on his right side. He no longer felt cold.

'Can you hear me, sir?' a deep voice asked.

Garet tried to answer but the result was hardly more than a whisper. His head seemed to be bandaged, and his chest.

'I think he's rejoined us, Mother,' the voice said. 'Praise the Lord.'

Garet tried to speak again, his whisper a little stronger.

'Who are you? Where am I?' The left side of his face tightened uncomfortably when he spoke. He opened his eyes, tried to focus.

'We are the Snow family,' the man said. 'We found you hurt at Ortega Lake and brought you home. Don't try to talk. Mother has some knuckle-broth for you. You've lost a lot of blood, and she says bone-marrow's the best for blood weakness. Brother Taylor, Nephi, I need your help, please?'

Garet felt three pairs of strong hands lift and turn him. A bearded face peered down at him.

'Now, sir. Mother Snow has broth for you.'

A plump woman with laughter-lines on her face pulled a stool up to the bed.

'Here, mister. This is good for what ails you.' She held a spoonful of broth to his lips. He slurped it into his mouth, spilling some down his chin. The woman promptly wiped it and ladled him another spoonful. The warm beefy taste seemed to give him strength, and his mouth opened eagerly as she ladled. And when Mother Snow brought a second bowl and he had consumed half of that, Garet felt that he might live.

'I'm Garet Havelock,' he said weakly. 'I have a spread on Silver Creek.'

'Pleased to meet you, Mr Havelock. I'm Bishop Harold Snow. This is Mother Snow, my wife Sarah, that is. And that's my neighbor Daniel Taylor and my son Nephi.'

'I owe you my life, Mr Snow.'

'We call him Bishop Snow,' Mother Snow said softly.

'Bishop Snow then.'

'The Lord giveth and the Lord taketh away,' said the bishop. 'If you owe your life, it's to him.' Then he said: 'Come in, children, and say hello to Mr Havelock.'

Ten young Snows swarmed in, ranging from four to about twenty. Bishop Snow introduced each one. Nephi was the eldest and Lam, who had first seen Garet at Ortega Lake, was the youngest.

Garet smiled at them, grateful for the reminder of warm family life.

'I'm afraid I need to ask you for one more favor, Bishop Snow.' Garet said. 'Could someone go to Rancho Pilar and tell them I'm alive?'

'I'll go,' Nephi volunteered.

'Now, children, brethren, stop pestering,' Mother Snow said. 'Mr Havelock's tuckered out and needs his rest.' The men left the room, followed by the children.

'Now you just get this broth down,' Mother Snow said, holding a spoonful to Garet's mouth. Garet finished the bowl and promptly fell asleep.

When he awoke he felt stronger. A swath of muslin bound his head. Another strip over the top of his head and under his jaw held a bandage to the left side of his face, the part that stretched painfully when he talked. His chest, too, was bound in muslin, and he could feel the pad it held in place against the painful wound beneath his shoulder-blade. Someone had dressed him in a pair of drawers, so his lower body was not naked. But abrasions along with painful soreness reminded him that he'd taken a tumble to the bottom of the canyon and been dragged by his horse all the way to Ortega Lake.

Mother Snow swept into the room with a platter of food.

'If you're awake, it's time to eat,' she declared, and proceeded to fill him with mashed potatoes, gravy, steamed squash, and ham-hock and beans all smashed up together. She topped the meal off with a large glass of buttermilk. Garet ate it all.

'Now, you get the urge, one way or the other, the chamber pot's under the bed,' Mother Snow said. 'You need the exercise so get out of bed somehow and do your own business.'

'Yes, ma'am.' Garet grinned. Mother Snow left.

Garet woke in the middle of the night with his bladder protesting. He managed to get to the floor, locate the pot, snatch the lid off, then sigh with relief as his urine sang against the porcelain vessel.

It was more difficult to push the pot back and worm his way into bed. But having accomplished it, he felt stronger. Again he slept.

Mother Snow greeted him in the morning with three eggs poached in milk and laid out on thick slices of toasted bread. She made him sit up and feed himself.

After clearing away his dishes, Mother Snow came in with a pile of clothes.

'I mended your shirt,' she said, 'and your pants . . . well, I did the best I could on patching them.'

'How long's it been now since you found me, Mother Snow?'

'Let me see, we went out to get crab-apples last Saturday.

126

That's when we found you. Today's Friday so it'll be a week tomorrow.'

A week. Someone had shot him out of the saddle with a small-caliber rifle. The same had happened to the *vaqueros* at Rancho Pilar. Maybe the same shooter. He had to get out of this bed and back on the dun.

'Thanks for the clothes, Mother Snow. I'll jump into them and ride out.'

'You'll do no such thing. The Pilars are sending a buggy for you tomorrow.'

'Mother Snow. I'm surely obliged. But could you call Bishop Snow?'

Mother Snow bustled out and returned with her husband.

'Mother Snow told me about the buggy, but I've got other places to go. Moving is the best way to get my body working, too. Now I'd be obliged if you'd saddle my dun.'

Seeing that Garet was determined to go, the bishop nodded.

'All right then. I'll help you get dressed.'

Even with the bishop's help it took a good portion of Garet's strength, but at last he sat on the edge of the bed in his neatly darned and patched clothes. He felt weak, but would his knee hold? Without the brace he might not be able to walk.

He sat on the edge of the bed and removed the muslin from his head and cheek. The lump on his head had subsided and the laceration was well scabbed over. Mother Snow's silk thread pulled the lips of the cut on his cheek together but the scar would zigzag across his face. The swelling and fever were gone from the wound, but the thread needed to stay.

Garet considered his situation. A bullet would have been quick and easy, so while someone wanted him dead, they also wanted him to suffer.

His fingers traced the healing wound on his face. And he remembered the two thin white scars on Laura's cheeks. Was

127

it the same person? Was he that close to the animal that abused his wife?

He seized the bedpost and pulled himself to his feet. The right leg stood all right, but the left wouldn't bear his weight.

'Bishop Snow, do you suppose you could find me something to use as a cane?'

'Surely.' The burly, bearded man soon returned with a juniper limb whittled into a rough cane.

With it Garet could take enough weight off his left knee to keep it from buckling.

'This's fine,' he said, hobbling into the Snows' front room. Nephi came in.

'The dun's saddled.'

Mother Snow held out a flour-sack.

'Sourdough bread and bacon,' she said. 'You must eat to regain your strength, Mr Havelock.'

'Mother Snow,' Garet said. 'You're an angel. I'll remember you as I eat.'

'You'll need this,' the bishop said, holding out a leather coat. 'Deerhide, it is, and lined with woven wool from the Navajo. Mother Snow made it.'

Garet was speechless. A week ago he was a stranger. Now, in addition to all their kindnesses, they give him a coat. He mumbled his thanks as he gingerly pulled the coat on. It fit perfectly.

'I'll try not to get bullet holes in it,' he said.

No one laughed.

Garet reached Silver Creek just after sunset. He saw that the framing of the new house had been completed and the ridge-pole raised. But he couldn't praise the work. He managed to stay aboard the dun until they reached the house, then toppled into Will's arms when he tried to dismount.

'Whoa there, cousin. You're weaker'n a day-old mouse.'

The men had built a bunkhouse east of the H-Cross ranch

house, and now they helped Garet toward it.

'Figured we'd better have some kind of shelter before winter,' Will explained.

Garet nodded. 'Good.'

A pot-bellied stove stood in the middle of the long room, which had six bunks built on to the walls. The men soon had a fire roaring and an extra bedroll laid out for Garet on one of the bunks.

'Damn bullet holes,' Garet muttered as he lay back so Will could pull off his boots.

Dan brought a plate of salt pork and beans with two big sourdough biscuits. Weak as he was, Garet found the food good and motioned for another helping as he finished the first. He sipped a cup of hot black coffee, sighing in appreciation.

After his second cup of coffee was poured Garet told the men his story.

'Damn.' Wont said. 'Bushwhacker. What kinda man's that?'

Then Garet told how the Snows found him.

'Someone had cut up my clothes, even my new sheepskin coat. And done away with my gun, my hat, and my brace. After all that he took a swipe at my face with a sharp knife.' Garet fingered the cut on his cheek. 'Will, think you can make me a new brace?'

'You tell me what you need and I'll make it. We got leather, and Wont's a pretty good hand with an awl.'

Garet explained how the brace worked.

'I can do that,' Will said, 'but it'll take a couple of days. You fort up here by the stove, eat when you're hungry, and sleep when you're tired. Just rest.'

Will Havelock was as good as his word and Garet soon had a new knee-brace to break in. Hoping extra rest would give the gunshot wound more time to heal, he spent much of the time asleep by the fire, safe while surrounded by kinfolk. But his waking hours were filled with thoughts of Laura and the child within her.

He broke in the brace by walking the creek-bank and the hill above the house, his breath white in the brisk November air. And he made trips to the low-hanging juniper to feed scraps to the brindle dog that made his home there. Sometimes he caught sight of it following him, keeping a safe distance and staying under cover. Once he found a quail laid in his path, the head neatly crushed by canine teeth. He built a small fire, skinned and skewered the bird, spit-roasted it, ate it, and left scraps for the dog.

Garet forced his muscles and scars to limber up by stretching. He twisted his torso left and right. He felt better, but he realized that complete recovery would be slow.

The gunshot wound began to close over and scab up in front. The larger exit-wound was raw and still leaked a little. Will helped him clean the wound. From the size of the entry-hole Garet figured he'd been hit by something less than .30-caliber. It would have been a long shot, too.

Most sharpshooters used .50-caliber rifles: Sharps or Remington Creedmores, like the ones at Hashknife headquarters. But Max Baker had convinced Garet that Hashknife was not behind the raids on Pilar sheep nor the attacks on Laura or himself . . . or the brindle dog.

Will proudly showed him every detail of the new house, its foundation stones, and ridge-pole construction. The rafters would soon be in place, to be covered with planks and topped with shingles split from native juniper.

The house made Garet lonely for Laura. It would be ready for her long before spring, and he wondered whether he'd be bringing one home to it, or two.

Dan Travis reported on the horses.

'Including the stallion,' he said, 'we've got thirty-eight head. The mares should give us another dozen or so next year, but maybe we should buy some broomtail colts to break and sell to the army.'

'Good job, Dan. We'll hold on the broomtails till spring. By then the Pilar trouble should be finished and I can help. You can keep your eyes peeled for a good milk-cow though. When Laura gets back the H-Cross will have to be a real ranch.

'I'll be riding for Concho in the morning,' Garet said. 'The dun should be rested up so I'll take him. I'll need that extra .44, too.'

Glancing into the mirror tacked above the commode, he noticed that the thin line of the knife-scar was still criss-crossed with Mother Snow's stitching.

'Dan, you got a sharp razor?'

'Why? You wanna shave?'

'I want you to cut these threads out of my face.'

Garet flinched every time Travis cut a thread and yanked it free, but daylight found Garet on his dun, riding toward Concho. While his strength was still far from normal and the wounds in his shoulder and back itched something fierce, he felt nearly human. Checking his back trail by habit, he noticed the dog. It seemed to be following, but kept far off to one side. Garet grinned.

'You follow me, brindle, you'll get yourself into trouble.'

CHAPTER THIRTEEN

When Ramon Javez brought news that Garet had ridden to Silver Creek, Laura stopped worrying. If he could ride he was recovering. But how did he feel about the baby? Would he forgive her? Garet was a man who did what was right. But would he accept the child? Would he be a loving father?

Laura, now in her sixth month of pregnancy, had outgrown the clothes Garet brought from Silver Creek. She had let out the seams, camouflaging the ill fit under a large apron, but soon she would need something made for women in late term. And she had nothing for the baby. No diapers. No little shirts and gowns. Suddenly, getting those things ready seemed urgent.

'Rita,' she confided, 'I'm growing out of my clothes. I need to make something more appropriate to my condition. I'd like to sew something, but I have no material. I thought maybe you might have some. Anything will do.'

'No, anything won't do. You must have two new dresses that are becoming to you. We must go to Señor Berado's store to choose some cloth.'

Laura gave her friend a frightened look.

'Oh, no . . .' Then she mustered her courage. 'I mean, yes, I'd like to do that. I want to get some soft cotton for baby-clothes and flannel for diapers, too.'

Rita smiled. 'Two of the women here are excellent seamstresses if you need help.'

Laura sobered. 'Rita, I have no money. If you will lend me enough for the materials I will pay you back as soon as I can.'

'Of course.'

Laura grasped her friend's hands.

'Please, can we go to Concho tomorrow?'

'*Sí*,' Rita said happily.

A single shot caught Garet's attention, and the three that followed in quick succession made him change direction. Someone was in trouble. The shots came from nearly due south. Garet could not ignore a call for help, but he let the dun pick his own way while he scanned the country. He didn't intend to ride into another dry-gulching.

As his eyes swept over the landscape Garet noticed the brindle dog, nearly a hundred yards off to the right.

Garet topped a low rise, and pulled up short. A horse was down and dead, with a man trapped unmoving under the carcass. A pistol lay nearby.

When Garet got closer, the man spoke.

'Havelock, you're a sight for sore eyes. Damn horse went down in a hole. Busted his leg all to hell. Mine too, for that matter. I had to shoot him, but he died right on top of me. Be obliged if you could get him off me.' Loren Buchard's breathing was labored.

Garet dismounted. He was in no shape to do heavy lifting, and the horse couldn't be rolled off.

'Mr Buchard. I don't see an easy way out of this. I'll look for something to pry up your horse so you can get out from under it. Any way you look at it, it's gonna hurt.'

'I've hurt before.'

Garet mounted the dun and rode to a stand of Utah juniper. There he cut a curving pole about four inches at the base and a little over two at the small end to use as a lever, then looked for a malpais rock that could serve as a fulcrum.

Not too big, or he couldn't carry it, but big enough to give the pole leverage. Buchard watched.

Favoring his wound, Garet found a rock he thought would do and rolled it next to the dead horse, then got the pole ready. He took his lariat from the dun's saddle, fixed its loop over the saddle horn of the dead horse, then backed the dun until the rope was taunt.

'Mr Buchard, I'm gonna have my dun tighten that rope while I put some weight on this lever. May let you pull your leg out.'

'You give me some space. I'll get the leg out.' Buchard clenched his teeth.

'Back, dun. Back,' Garet called. The horse lowered his haunches and backed up with stiff front legs. Buchard's dead horse rolled a little, and Garet jammed his lever just behind the shoulder, as close to Buchard's leg as he dared.

'Back, dun.'

The dun again budged the carcass, while Garet put his weight on the lever. Then, with the dun holding, Garet repositioned his pole.

'I think we'll get a little space this time, Mr Buchard. You get ready to pull. Back, dun.'

Buchard grunted, put the boot of his good leg against the dead horse and pushed. The trapped leg slid free. He inched away from the carcass, then lay with his eyes closed, chest heaving and face deathly white. Sweat beaded his brow.

'Dun, here.' On Garet's command the horse walked forward.

'Mr Buchard,' Garet said. 'I got shot a couple of weeks ago, so I can't lift worth a lick. I'm going to make a travois to haul you with. It'll take a while. Likely as not we'll have to spend the night out here.'

'Do what you have to.'

Garet got his bedroll and rolled Buchard in the blankets.

'I'll gather wood and get poles cut while it's still light.'

For firewood Garet, with help from the dun, dragged two juniper deadfalls close to where Buchard lay. For the travois he cut two green juniper poles about twelve feet long.

The night was cold so Garet spent most of it feeding branches from the deadfalls into the fire, keeping the flames high. Once he noticed the eyes of the brindle dog reflecting the light, but the animal kept his distance. At dawn Garet set to work on the travois, using Buchard's lariat and saddle blanket to make the litter. He rigged the travois on the dun by hanging the pole-ends from behind his own saddle's cantle with Buchard's surcingle.

Once everything was set Garet pulled a biscuit and some cold bacon from his saddle-bags. He offered to share, but Buchard couldn't eat.

'Just get me home,' he murmured. His face was flushed and hot.

Garet laid the travois flat next to Buchard, with the rancher still wrapped in blankets, then rolled him on to the travois.

After resting a few minutes Garet tied Buchard to the travois, hitched it to the dun, mounted, and set off toward the Forty-Four.

Late in the morning Dick Blasingame came riding toward them, head down, watching Buchard's tracks. Garet hailed and he came at a gallop.

'His leg's broke and he's got a fever, Blas,' Garet said. 'Could you hightail it to Show Low and fetch Doc Wolford. I'll get Buchard to the Forty-Four.'

'All right, Havelock. You just keep that man alive.'

'It'll take more than a travois ride to kill Loren Buchard,' Garet said.

Blasingame left at a lope. Garet's dun kept pulling the travois. Once in a while Garet dismounted to check on Buchard. The rancher's cheeks were burning hot and his breathing shallow, but he was still alive when Garet brought the travois to the back door of the Forty-Four ranch house. A

135

light glowed in the kitchen.

'Hello the house,' Garet shouted. The cook opened the door. 'Come help me, Cookie. Mr Buchard's got a busted leg, and we need to get him into bed.'

'For God's sake,' Buchard moaned. When the travois lay on the ground, Garet had the cook saw off the long ends of the poles. 'I got me a gunshot wound, Cookie, so let's just take 'er easy.'

Garet and Cookie carefully maneuvered the rancher into his bedroom. Buchard cried out as they rolled him out of the blankets and on to the bed.

The cook lit a coal-oil lamp.

'Much obliged to you, Havelock.'

'Mind if I stay till the doc gets here?' Garet asked. Buchard seemed to have passed out.

The cook went out, returning shortly with coffee and a plate of doughnuts.

'Never saw a man but what didn't feel better after a little bear sign,' he said.

Garet agreed, munching on one, washing the sweetness down with the strong coffee. It was like a second lease on life.

The doughnuts were gone when Doc Wolford bustled into the room with Blasingame close behind.

'Now get out of here and let me work,' he ordered. Blasingame led Garet back to the dining-room where the cook set another plate of doughnuts between them.

'You knew I got dry-gulched, didn't you, Blas?'

'Yeah, I heard.' Blasingame's mouth was full of doughnut. 'Bad?'

'I'd not be here if it weren't for the Bishop Snow and his wife over to Obed.'

'Any idea who it was?'

'No. But he shot from far off and I'd guess the gun was no more'n .25- caliber.'

Blasingame closely inspected his third doughnut.

'Ain't too many small-caliber rifles like that,' he said quietly.

'You know something, Blas?'

'I can't say, Havelock. I just can't say.'

Doc Wolford came in.

'Got his leg splinted. Gave him some laudanum for pain. He'll be fine.' Wolford handed Blasingame a small bottle of whitish liquid. 'Here's more laudanum if he gets to hurting. But don't give him any if he doesn't ask.'

'Gotcha, Doc. Thanks.'

As the doctor was leaving he turned to Blasingame.

'By the way, where is young Rafe?' he asked.

'Not right sure, Doc.'

'Well, you tell him there's a turkey-shoot on Saturday. Likely he'll want to get his share with that little Marlin .25-25 of his.

'Marlin .25-25?' Garet said, his eyes on Dick Blasingame.

Laura's stomach fluttered at the thought of venturing outside Rancho Pilar, but she was determined to conquer her fear. Rita's tap came at the door.

'The buggy is ready.'

'I'll be right there.' Laura pulled on her sun-bonnet, then put the Colt Lightning in her pocket. She was ready.

'Laura. You look wonderful.' Rita clasped her friend's hands. 'But it is cold today. Please take this wrap of Pilar wool. And we'll use a lap-robe as well.'

Matched grays were hitched to the buggy, their breath white in the chill air. Ramon helped Laura into the vehicle. Rita got in the other side, took the reins with practiced hands, and clucked the team through the main gate and on toward Concho.

The sound of running horses came from behind, and two Pilar *vaqueros* took positions on either side of the buggy, riding with rifles resting on their thighs like lances.

'Could we stop at the chapel?' Laura asked as they neared the mission. Rita reined up and both women went in. Laura felt strange entering God's house with the pistol in her pocket, but she wanted to feel once again the peace she had experienced there. She genuflected before the image of the Blessed Virgin, then prayed for Garet's safe return.

Rita handed her a candle.

'Let us light candles for our men,' she whispered. They lit their candles from the flames of those already burning and placed them in supplication.

'What brings two beautiful daughters of God to our humble mission?' Padre Bautista asked.

'Prayers, of course.' Rita smiled at the padre, but Laura was concerned that she had not heard him approach. Such carelessness could get me killed, she thought, and vowed to be more aware.

'It is good to see you outside the hacienda, Laura.'

'Thank you, Padre.'

'We are going to Señor Berado's store to purchase some wonderful cloth,' Rita said. 'Laura needs new dresses.'

Padre Bautista accompanied the women to the buggy, bidding them: 'Go with God.'

Laura chose yardage, lace, and ribbons from Berado's limited stock in less than an hour.

'Is there anything else you want?' Rita asked. Laura shook her head. She wanted to be back inside the walls of Rancho Pilar as soon as possible.

About half-way home the outriding *vaqueros* peeled off to intercept an oncoming rider. Then they fell in on either side and escorted him to the buggy. Laura's heart leapt into her throat when she recognized her Garet.

Dick Blasingame had shown Garet the gun-cabinet after Doc Wolford left. It held six rifles, two of which were sharpshooter guns. One was a Sharps .50 and the other a Marlin .25-25.

'Young Rafe favors the little gun,' Blasingame said. 'And he can take the head off a turkey a quarter of a mile away.'

Garet said nothing, but the rifle was convincing evidence. Loren Buchard was groggy from the laudanum, so Garet had to leave the Forty-Four without talking to either him or Rafe.

The pieces were falling in place. The Pilar men wounded by small-caliber sniping. The knife cut across his own face. The scars on Laura's cheeks. The secret of Rafe's mother. Things pointed at Rafe Buchard, not only as the ringleader of those who attacked the Pilars, but also as the one who had shot and cut Garet, raped and cut Laura.

'Ladies.' Garet tipped his hat and offered a small smile to Laura. Then he kneed the dun ahead and took the point. The Pilar riders rode out on either side of the buggy accompanying it to safety within the walls of Rancho Pilar.

A short while later Ness Havelock too rode through the main gate. Garet met him at the corral.

'How's it going, big brother?'

'Other than getting shot, I guess I'm all right.'

'Shot!'

Garet filled Ness in on what had happened.

'And I have me a hunch that Rafe Buchard has a lot of explaining to do.'

Ness nodded. 'Tom sent a message,' he said. 'He's staying with Alchesay's White Mountain Apaches, and says the Jicarilla from Puma's band has something to show you on East Fork.'

'What?'

'Don't know. Said you'd want to see it. But with you shot up, you'd better let me ride along. The woollies are down the mountain and Miguel and the *vaqueros* will be plenty of protection here.'

'All right. Have Rita rustle us up some grub. I'll say a word to Laura. Then we'll move out.'

Garet found Laura in her room. She looked startled

when she saw him, and a little afraid. They stood for a moment searching each other's face. Neither could find words. Then Garet stepped across the void and took her in his arms.

'It's all right, Laura,' he murmured. 'Everything's all right.'

Laura felt her heart would burst.

'Oh, Garet, I need you.'

'I know, honey. I need you, too. Even more than I realized.' He kissed her, and she clung to his kiss, desperate for assurance that he also loved the child.

'Honey, Ness has brought word that Tom Morgan wants me up on East Fork. I got to go.'

She staggered back.

'But Garet . . . Your wound . . . Can't someone else. . . ?'

'Tom says the Jicarilla has found something. Now we may be able to trace the man who . . . the man who attacked you. I've got to do it, Laura. I can't rest till he's caught.' Again he held her close. 'You'll be safe here.'

Laura nodded, tears in her eyes. She stood on tiptoe to kiss the scar on his cheek.

'Take care, my love,' she said. 'If anything happens to you, I'll die.'

'No. You won't die.' Garet spoke tenderly. 'You'll live. And, Laura, you'll be the best mother a kid could have.' He kissed the tears streaming down her scarred cheeks.

Then he was gone.

The brothers camped the first night near an overhanging cliff, using it to reflect warmth from their fire, and took turns sleeping and watching.

East Fork ran into White River, south of Old Baldy. The horsemen took the pass, dropped into Horseshoe Ciénaga, and built a smoke. Two hours later Tom Morgan rode in on his mule. The Jicarilla accompanied him on foot.

'Howdy, Tom. Chiwadne got something?'

'He does. Shall we ride?'

The Jicarilla moved ahead, leading them up toward the flank of Mount Ord. The East Fork, over the eons, had cut deep into the earth, and the riders were often far above the streambed. Then the Jicarilla halted and motioned for them to come on foot.

Chiwadne led them to a ravine where there had been a small landslide. The Apache pointed to a spot below where the stiff leg of a dead horse jutted from the rubble. He spoke briefly to Morgan, who translated.

'He says that horse was tied out behind your cabin, Havelock.'

Garet went slipping and sliding down the ravine. At the bottom, he could see there wasn't much left but hide and bones. The Apache showed Garet the right rear hoof and its distinctive shoe which had left the prints at Silver Creek.

'Come down here,' Garet called. 'Let's unbury this cayuse.'

The four men moved boulders and rocks, branches and dirt. At last the carcass was uncovered; a paint horse that had once been a stallion. Besides the tell-tale hind-hoof they saw no other mark.

'Let's turn it over,' Ness said. 'There may be a brand.' They attached their lariats over the front and back feet, but when they tried to roll the carcass it came apart, leaving ribs and hide stuck to the ground. Garet edged his Bowie under the hide, prying it up from the ground. When he peeled it back, high on the right shoulder he found a 44 brand. The stallion had belonged to Loren Buchard.

'By God. It's Rafe Buchard. That's who's done all this.' Garet cut away a square of hide with the brand on it. 'Now I've got proof.'

Back out of the ravine, Garet thanked Morgan, who elected to stay with the Apaches. Chiwadne left too, after Garet promised to visit Chief Puma.

'Come on, Ness. I got a man to see.' Garet stuffed the piece of hide into his saddle-bags and mounted the dun.

As the brothers dropped into Sheep's Crossing headed for Lee Valley, the first snowflakes began to fall.

CHAPTER FOURTEEN

The Havelocks rode on through the deepening snow, hoping they wouldn't have to fort up. But long before they reached the north end of Lee Valley the snow fell too thick and fast for them to see more than a few feet. The wind grew stronger and the men paused to tie bandannas over their Stetsons.

'Ness, I'm about done in,' Garet called. 'We only got a couple of hours of daylight. Best we find a place to wait this storm out.'

The snow fell in large, soft flakes that piled up quickly. With visibility getting worse, the whole land was rapidly turning into a white cloud with no sense of depth or direction. They let the horses have their heads, hoping they were going steadily north-west toward the flanks of Old Baldy, but as the snow thickened the horses moved more and more slowly, often shaking their heads to dislodge the white coatings on their eyelashes and forelocks. Away from the open grassland at the bottom of the valley the dun took the lead, breaking trail in the deep snow among fir and spruce trees, weaving through stands of quaking aspen.

The wind howled from the south, caking the heavy snow against the riders' backs. In a big stand of bare-branched aspen Garet signaled for a halt.

'This wind ain't gonna let up,' he shouted. 'Better stop here and put up a lean-to.'

Ness slid from his saddle.

'You get behind the horses. I'll find a spot.' He took his lariat and looped it over the stump of a fallen aspen. It would give him fifty feet to explore. He soon returned.

'Follow me,' he shouted. With Garet holding on to the bay's tail and leading the dun, Ness led the bay to where he had picked two trees about ten feet apart. One had a double trunk that would hold poles. They could use a lariat to hold them to the other tree-trunk. Young growth was thick so it wasn't long until they had a stack of poles cut with their sharp Bowies to make a wall about five feet high, which blocked the wind-driven snow.

They still had daylight, but the air was getting colder and, while their coats kept their torsos warm, their hands and feet were hurting. Garet led the horses to the sheltered side of the wall and tied them, then sat down out of the wind while Ness used the lariat lifeline to scout for trees suitable to cut for the lean-to. He brought back a small deadfall pine to use for a fire as well. Garet hacked off small branches with his Bowie, then slanted his knife left and right to cut chips from the resinous trunk. Once started, pitchy pine would burn through any high wind.

The cold ate at Garet's fingers, making it hard to hold a knife, but at last he had the makings ready. He scraped snow from the lean-to to clear a fire-bed at the east end, then laid the fire carefully. But when he struck the first lucifer the wind promptly snuffed it out. He sheltered the second with his body, but it burned only until he tried to move it to the wood and shavings and once more the wind blew it out. He went to his saddle-bags and got the square of horsehide. Two more tries using the horsehide as a windbreak and the pine shavings caught. In a few moments the flames licked high. Garet shoved the end of the tree-trunk into the fire, to be moved into the lean-to as it burned.

Ness had finished the roof so that it projected over the

horses, and formed a shelter for the men. He lugged in the saddles and saddle-bags, stacking them in one open end, then tied a saddle blanket with pigging-strings to complete the enclosure. The wind howled at them and blew flakes of snow in through the woven roof but as the snow piled up on the withes it stopped sifting in.

Even the brindle dog wormed his way in out of the storm, shaking the snow off his coat and crawling into the lowest part of the lean-to, where he lay facing the fire. A little later Garet noticed a snowshoe rabbit the dog had dropped next to the saddles.

Ness got a small coffee-pot from his saddle-bag and filled it with snow. He placed it at the edge of the fire and added more snow as it melted until he had enough to make coffee. Soon the aroma of fresh coffee filled the lean-to. Ness tapped the side of the pot to settle the grounds and poured a cup for Garet, another for himself.

'All the comforts of home,' he said, raising his cup in a salute.

'Yeah. Long as we can keep the fire going.' Garet took a sip of the hot, black brew. 'But it sure hits the spot, don't it?' He grinned at Ness. 'You sleep first. I'll tend the fire.'

They put down the tarp ground-cloths from their bedrolls to keep the cold and moisture from coming through. Ness removed neither boots nor coat, but cocooned himself in blankets and pillowed his head on a pair of saddle-bags.

At daybreak snow was still falling though the wind had died. It continued all day, and to find firewood the brothers had to make another lifeline with two lariats tied together. When the second day dawned crisp and clear they saddled up and started out through the deep, powdery snow. The dog disappeared, preferring his own trail.

When they came to the mail road at the north end of the valley they followed it east, then dropped off the heights at Mormon Bend and made their way toward Round Valley.

The ring of mountains had contained the storm, and the brothers rode into Round Valley with just a bit of daylight remaining. The town corral had a ramshackle stable where they put their horses, grateful that the hostler had oats for sale. Cash. They stayed the night above the saloon, and rode out after breakfast.

'You don't seem happy,' Ness said as they left.

'I was thinking about Buchard. He's a good man and a good neighbor and I'm going after his only son. That's not a good feeling, Ness.'

'Don't see that we have a choice.'

'Yeah. Might as well get it over with.' Garet kneed the dun into a canter toward the Forty-Four, where an old man lay abed and a rapist and killer walked free.

As they rode Garet's rage began to build. What kind of animal was Rafe Suchard? Raiding sheep camps. Killing herders. Attacking Rancho Pilar. Shooting people from ambush. And now, with the damning horsehide from that pinto stallion bearing the Forty-Four brand, he knew that Rafe Suchard had attacked Laura. Must have. He was the one, all right, the one who had fathered the child Laura would bear. Garet bit his lip until the salty taste of blood filled his mouth.

A mile from the Forty-Four ranch house they stopped to wait for nightfall, so the cowboys would be in the bunkhouse. The dog lay down to rest beneath a juniper.

At dark they walked their horses forward. Lights showed in the ranch house and the bunkhouse. Horses stood in the corral and one was tied to the hitching-rail. Garet and Ness shucked their Winchesters. Ness peeled off toward the bunkhouse.

Garet waited until Ness had entered the bunkhouse and no shots were fired. Then he dismounted the dun, got the horse-hide swatch from his saddle-bags, and shoved it behind his belt in back. He stepped quietly on to the porch, then lunged into the kitchen.

'Easy, Cookie, and you won't get hurt.'

The cook stood with hands high, eyes wide with fear.

'I ain't no fighter, Havelock. Ain't no gun in my kitchen.'

'I'm after Rafe,' Garet said, motioning toward the front room. 'You go in there and call him. Don't try anything. I'm right behind you.'

The cook, swallowing hard, nodded, then moved into the front room with Garet a step behind.

'Mr Rafe. Mr Rafe!'

Rafe's reply came from the back of the house.

'Waddaya want?'

Garet's anger made a hard lump in his chest at the sound of Rafe's voice. He prodded the cook with the Winchester.

'What's the matter, Cookie?' Loren Buchard called from his bedroom.

'Mr Rafe?' The cook squeaked. 'Come here, Mr Rafe. Please.' Footsteps sounded on the wooden floor, and Rafe Buchard appeared.

'Rafe!' Garet shouted, aiming the Winchester at him.

'Run, Mr Rafe.' The cook plowed into Garet, knocking the Winchester aside and almost upsetting him. Rafe disappeared down the hall.

Garet, ignoring the cook, jerked out his Colt and dashed down the hallway as fast as his limp would allow. Rafe ducked into his father's room.

'Rafe. What's going on?' Loren Buchard sat in bed, his broken leg propped up.

Rafe struggled with the window as Garet rushed in. Garet fired a warning shot into the ceiling, and Rafe, hands above his head, cringed against the wall.

Buchard glared at Garet.

'Havelock, you better have a good reason for barging in on a neighbor with your gun in hand.' His voice was hard and full of gravel.

'Mr Buchard, I came after your boy. With proof.'

147

'Show me,' the father demanded.

Rafe slumped into a dejected pile beneath the windowsill.

'Your son's the one behind the raids on Pilar sheep,' Garet said, 'and two herders are dead. He led the attack on Rancho Pilar. Used Giant Powder to blow the wall. But he started it by sniping at *vaqueros* with his Marlin.'

'Yes. *Yes*! I did.' Rafe screamed. 'And I'd do it again. Those Pilars cheated my mother. She always said they turned her out with nothing, when they had a roomful of gold. I want my share!'

'You shot me, too,' Garet continued.

'Yes. I shot you. You should be dead.'

Garet fingered the scar on his face. 'It seems you just naturally like to cut folks.'

Rafe's lip curled. 'Some deserve to die slow. You, for one. Like a dog, I say.'

'I've seen what you do to dogs, too.' Garet had to resist smashing the sneer from Rafe's face with the barrel of his .44.

Buchard spoke then, his voice weary.

'You are wrong, son. When your mother left the Pilars they gave her more gold than you can imagine. How do you think the Forty-Four got to be like it is? It was a rawhide outfit before she came, but with her dowry from Don Fernando we made big changes.'

Rafe seemed incredulous.

'Don't lie to me!' he cried. 'She said . . .'

'I know. Your mother said things. But what I say is true.'

'Can't be!' Rafe jumped to his feet.

'Don't do it.' Garet centered the Colt on Rafe's chest.

'Big man, Havelock. Wish to God you'd died.'

Garet grabbed Rafe by the front of his shirt and twisted it into a choke-hold.

'You're not man enough to kill me, Rafe. Or my wife.'

'What about your wife?'

'You attacked her in my cabin, that's what.' In his anger

Garet forgot about his half-healed wounds, he forgot about everything but getting revenge on the cur who'd harmed Laura. His iron grip pinned Rafe against the wall.

'Havelock, you've got it all wrong.' A look of pain clouded Buchard's face. 'Rafe doesn't like women. Never has. I mean . . . what I'm saying is that Rafe would never lie with a woman. That's just not in his make-up.'

Garet glared at Buchard, grasping his words. Then he holstered the Colt, yanked the square of horsehide from his belt and brandished it at Buchard.

'This horse was tied to a juniper behind my cabin. The sign said the man riding it hurt my Laura. Look. A pinto stallion wearing a Forty-Four brand. Now tell me that Rafe didn't attack my wife!'

Rafe stared at the horsehide swatch. But it was Loren Buchard who spoke up.

'Why, that's the horse Dick Blasingame favored,' he exclaimed. 'Where'd you find it?'

Buchard's words hit Garet like a sledge-hammer.

'Blasingame?' He released his grip on Rafe's shirt. He couldn't connect the good-natured foreman with the cruel assault on Laura. But there it was.

'My God!' he murmured. 'Blasingame.' He straightened, then drew his Colt again. 'Mr Buchard, Rafe's done what he's done. I got to turn him over to Sheriff Hubbell. You can see that, can't you?'

Buchard nodded, his face haggard with sadness.

'Your son is responsible for dead men and slaughtered sheep,' Garet said. 'Ness will take him to Saint Johns tomorrow and turn him over to Sheriff Hubbell. I'll go after Dick Blasingame.'

Garet took another handful of Rafe's shirt and pulled him in close.

'Now tell me,' he growled. 'What did you do with Pablo's head?'

149

Rafe scowled. 'Who's Pablo?'

'He's the sheepherder you and your boys shot during the second raid.'

Rafe shrugged. 'Dunno.'

Garet tightened his grip on Rafe's shirt.

'A widow woman and two children didn't get a last look at their man because he didn't have a head. Now someone in your bunch cut that herder's head off and hid it. You tell me where.'

Rafe tried to push Garet away. Garet merely shook him again.

'Tell me!'

Rafe sputtered.

'I dunno of any head. Didn't see no one do it. That's the honest truth.'

Garet gave Rafe a searching look.

'All right.' He released his grip and Rafe fell back against the wall. 'If you're lying, you'll answer to me.' Garet turned to Buchard. 'Where's Blasingame live?' he asked.

'He's got a homestead in Randall Ciénaga up toward Wolf Mountain. Follow the ridgeline from here for about five miles.'

In the cold of the early morning after fitful sleep in the barn, Garet rose, saddled the dun and mounted up. The big brindle dog stood just outside the stable door, watching. Garet checked the action of his guns, then set off for Blasingame's homestead.

CHAPTER FIFTEEN

Laura counted the days. It was almost December and Garet had been gone too long. The baby inside her grew more active with each passing day, impatient, Laura thought, to escape its confines. Laura's doubts of Garet's acceptance of the child grew, too. She could not forget his stricken face when he realized the child was not his. By now he has had time to realize that this child is ours, she thought. We will bring it into the world, we will raise it, and we will be proud of its growth and accomplishments. In time we will love it as we love each other. Could the simple miracle she visualized actually come to pass? Yes, with love it could. Her love for Garet. Her love for the child. Her love would envelop the three of them.

The hacienda lay silent under the starry midnight sky. Laura snuffed out the candle and slipped beneath the heavy quilts. She stared at the ceiling. The baby, too, was restless, stretching and turning, kicking into her side.

Suddenly sunlight streamed through the window, and Laura realized she had slept.

'Laura, wake up, you sleepy head.' Rita's laughter came from beyond the oak door. 'Breakfast is ready. And a new day is here, a wonderfully bright new day. Come on, get up! Get up!'

'I'm up.' Laura dressed quickly in the cold room, washed her face, combed her hair, and went to see what awaited her at the Pilar breakfast table.

'Let us be thankful for what God gives us,' Don Fernando said, and everyone began to eat.

*

With the sunrise Garet's dun picked its way up the ciénaga toward Blasingame's homestead. His turned-up coat collar warmed his neck and ears, and doeskin gloves kept his hands comfortable, his right resting on his thigh, inches from the butt of his Colt, his left reining in the dun as he approached the dugout.

'Dick Blasingame,' Garet shouted, pulling his Colt.

After a few moments Blasingame opened the door.

'What'd ya want, Havelock?' Then seeing the Colt, 'What's the gun for?' He stepped out, pulling the door shut behind him.

'Blas, what happened to that pinto stallion you used to ride?'

A flicker of uneasiness crossed Blasingame's eyes, but he answered in his customary level tone. 'That horse was stole, Havelock. Why?'

Garet pulled the swatch of horsehide from under his coat with his left hand.

'A Jicarilla Apache friend of mine found that horse's carcass up on East Fork. Nothing much left but hide and bones. And this brand.'

Blasingame scowled at the scrap of hide.

'And you know what, the right hind-hoof of that horse matched tracks at my cabin on Silver Creek where someone raped my wife!' Garet's voice rose. His face reddened with rage. 'Blasingame. That man was you!'

Blasingame's gaze held Garet's fierce black eyes.

'Could've been anyone, Havelock. Like I said, the paint was stole.'

Garet clenched his teeth.

'Blas. Don't you mess with me. I won't stand for it.'

A mewling sound came from inside the dugout.

'OK, Havelock,' Blasingame said quickly. 'I'll get my coat and come with you. We can get this thing straightened out.'

152

Garet seethed with rage. But there was just enough doubt in his mind for him to allow the foreman to step back into the dugout. Garet waited. But Blasingame didn't come out.

'Blas,' he called.

No answer.

'Blas, come out or I'm coming in.'

Silence.

Garet dismounted, Colt in hand. At the door he stood to one side in case Blasingame shot through the pine boards. From inside he heard that strange mewling sound.

He tried the door. It was latched from the inside. He stepped back and lunged, striking the pine door with his right shoulder and arm. It burst inward.

A double bed stood against the back wall. Above it hung Pablo's head. It looked smoked like a ham. Only now the sightless eyes stared down at a naked woman tied spread-eagled on the bed. The mewling sounds came from her ruined face.

Garet holstered his Colt and covered the woman with a blanket, then cut her bonds with his Bowie.

'You're safe now, ma'am. I'm going after Blasingame, and I'll make sure he never touches you again.' Her eyes wide with terror, the woman clutched the blanket to her.

In inspecting a burlap-covered opening on the back wall Garet discovered a tunnel. He found a flour-sack, cut down the head, and placed it in the sack and out of sight in the tunnel. Blasingame was sicker than Garet had ever imagined. The tunnel ran from the dugout to a wash near the corrals. It had taken only moments for Blasingame to escape.

Garet mounted the dun and struck out on Blasingame's trail. Several times he lost the trail on rocky ground and had to cast around to find it again. Then he noticed the dog up ahead. The brindle was also casting back and forth. Eventually it trotted off in a straight line, looking back over its shoulder to see if Garet was following.

Garet decided to bet on the dog. He urged the dun into a

canter, and the dog lined out ahead.

When Blasingame's trail turned toward Wolf Mountain, Garet urged his horse into a gallop, hoping to catch the rapist before he reached the cliffs at the mountain's foot. The brindle raced out on the flat, headed full speed for the malpais cliffs. A sudden puff of smoke, then the report of a rifle told Garet he'd caught up with his quarry. The dog ran on.

Garet stopped the dun and ground-tied him behind a screen of junipers. He pulled a pair of moccasins from the saddle-bags and put them on. On the malpais they were surer and quieter than boots.

Another rifle report came from the cliffs. Blasingame hadn't moved. Garet faded into the junipers. Slowly he worked his way up into the rocks above the cliffs. The dog scrambled over and among the boulders. Blasingame took two shots at it, but the dog went on.

Some distance above the cliff-line Garet came upon a cave. Could be Blasingame was heading for it.

Another rifle shot sounded. Closer. Garet heard Blasingame curse.

'This time I'll kill you, you mangy cur!'

Garet waited out of sight near the mouth of the cave. Then Blasingame came into view, climbing up the slope and watching over his shoulder.

'Hello, Blas.' When Garet spoke the foreman dropped behind the clutter of malpais.

'Blas, you can't get away from me. I saw what you did to your wife. I know you're the one who abused my Laura.'

Blasingame snapped a shot, but Garet had dropped back among the rocks.

'So you saw, did you?' Blasingame spoke in his level, almost emotionless voice. 'Well, Havelock, a little pain makes women do exactly what you want them to. That Mex wife of mine's meek. Does just what I say. No talking back. That's what pain applied just right does. Works every time. With dogs, too, and horses . . . and sometimes men.'

Garet wanted to keep him talking.

'Might not always work, Blas.' He started a flanking move-ment, slipping through the malpais softly, slowly, with great care.

'Now your Laura's a fine-looking woman.' Blasingame laughed. 'And there she was. By herself and lonesome like. Seemed natural that I pay her a social call. That Laura of yours, mighty willing . . . after some pain, that is.'

Garet's rage nearly blinded him. He could stand no more. He jumped up and shouted.

'Here I am, bastard!'

Blasingame swung his rifle frantically as Garet triggered his Colt. The first bullet caught Blasingame just above the right hip, and his shot went wide. Garet's second shot fractured the stock of Blasingame's Winchester and ricocheted up his fore-arm, smashing bone and tearing muscle and sinew.

Before Garet could thumb back his Colt's hammer again, the big brindle dog sprang at Blasingame's neck. A scream of terror faded into a gurgle as the rapist tumbled to the ground. The dog growled, shaking his head as he sent his fangs deeper, severing the carotid arteries. The larynx collapsed, cutting off the panicked gurgling sounds. Blasingame's body heaved and shook and his heels beat on the ground.

Garet lunged for the dog, but before he could pull him off, Blasingame was dead.

Laura shaded her eyes and squinted, trying to see who the two approaching riders were. Soon she saw that one was Garet. The other, wrapped in a wool trade blanket which formed a hood, was a woman.

Laura ran to the front gate. Her man had come home, that was what mattered. Garet kept the horses at a slow, easy walk. A brindle dog trotted along behind.

To Laura it seemed an eternity before Garet and the woman rode through the gate. Laura ran to the dun and clutched Garet's leg.

'Oh, Garet. Thank God, you're safe.'

He looked at her with eyes full of sadness.

'I'm safe, Laura, and so are you. This ordeal is over for us. But I'm afraid not for her.' He nodded toward the bundled woman.

Paloma and Rita appeared on the veranda as Garet dismounted and handed the reins to one of the boys. Garet grasped the waist of the blanket-wrapped woman, and she slid from the saddle into his arms. The blanket fell away from her ruined face.

Rita gasped. 'Luciana.'

'Take her to my room,' Laura said. 'She'll feel safe there.'

Garet carried Luciana Blasingame in, gently placed her on Laura's bed, and left. Laura winced as she removed the blanket and bloody tattered skirt. Rita came with the medicine-box, Paloma fetched a basin of hot water, and the women began their ministrations.

Garet, trailed by the brindle dog, rode into Silver Creek nearly a week after the death of Dick Blasingame. For the first time in months his mind did not fester with thoughts of Laura's attacker. The man with the twisted mind now lay in a shallow grave near that hell-hole dugout.

He saw the roofed house from nearly a mile away. The juniper shingles shone bright above the fresh pine logs, and a wisp of smoke curled from the kitchen's stovepipe chimney. The scene brought a smile of pride and contentment to Garet's face, not only at having a real home on a full-fledged ranch, but at having cousins, family, to help out.

'Hello the house,' he shouted as he reined up in the yard.

Will and Wont both came to the door, which was still just a framed hole in the log walls.

'What'll ya take for the house?' Garet asked.

Wont's face was completely sober as he said,

'Sorry, mister. This house ain't for sale. It belongs to a lady name of Laura Havelock.'

Garet chuckled. 'Mighty fine job,' he said.

'Right now the front room's our carpenter shop where we're making the little stuff. Shutters. Doors. Some kitchen shelves. Figured we might as well make an icebox, too. We made enough sawdust in that saw pit for you to have an ice-cave.'

'I'd sure like to bring Laura home at Christmas. Think it'll be ready by then?'

The Havelock cousins grinned.

'We'll have it ready.'

Garet moved his things into the bunkhouse, then pitched in, doing what he could to help out. The brindle dog took up residence under the bunkhouse steps. Three days before Christmas the house was ready – except for curtains, rugs, and other such comforts that Laura would want to supervise. Garet saddled up to go fetch her.

Laura, looking prettier than ever, ran into Garet's arms when he arrived. Her belly was large now, but he gathered woman and child to him, vowing they would never again be apart. The hacienda was festive with Christmas candles and the fragrance of spruce.

When everyone gathered around the big table for supper Garet made his announcement.

'Don Fernando, you've sheltered my wife all these months, for which I will always be indebted. Rita, you've been a good friend to my Laura. And Miguel, *mi amigo*, a good neighbor. Thank you.'

Miguel raised his glass in salute.

'Now if you'll put up with us a little longer,' Garet continued, 'I'll take Laura home to Silver Creek on Christmas Day.'

Laura gasped. Silver Creek! For an instant, panic rose in her throat. Then she steeled herself. She'd go. Blasingame was dead. She smiled up at Garet, and he returned the smile with loving eyes.

Miguel grinned broadly.

'My friends,' he said. 'Laura has accumulated many possessions. I think we must take a wagon to carry them all. And we must use the buggy for her comfort. Therefore, it would be best if the Pilars accompanied with a few *vaqueros* to guard everything.'

Everyone cheered. Except Rita.

'Rita,' Garet said, 'you have been more than a friend to Laura. You are the sister I never had.'

Rita burst into tears.

'Garet!' Laura scolded. 'Ness left without a word. All his things are gone. Rita thinks he might not come back.'

Garet's face turned serious.

'I don't know where he's gone, but he'll be back. One thing I do know. Rita, you're the woman he wants.'

Rita searched Garet's eyes.

'I had hoped someday to be his wife.'

'If I know my brother, you will be,' Garet said.

Ramon stomped in from outside.

'We shall have snow for Christmas,' he announced.

The snow fell lightly the next morning, but little had accumulated on the ground. Laura packed while Garet made plans with Don Fernando and Miguel. Rita, in better spirits, fetched some large baskets and an old trunk in which to transport Laura's things.

Laura didn't see a wagon leave the *rancho* for Silver Creek, laden with a haunch of beef and baskets of vegetables and baked goods.

That evening, her packing complete, Laura joined the others in a Christmas Eve supper that included sweetmeats and cider. Then she and Garet went with the Pilars to the mission's midnight Christmas mass.

After a few hours' sleep and a hearty Christmas breakfast an impressive procession left the hacienda. Rita and Laura drove the Pilar buggy. Garet rode his dun at the left front wheel, Laura's mare Mandy tied on behind. Another Pilar wagon followed, carrying Laura's things, along with several Pilar women and children, hidden by the wagon's canvas top.

Two Pilar *vaqueros* rode on each side of the little caravan, the great silver rowels on their spurs jingling gaily. Don Fernando and Miguel rode at the head of the procession, mounted on matching golden palominos, whose pale manes and tails glowed in the early light. Miguel carried a flag that bore the Pilar family emblem, a hawk in flight.

The sun was high overhead when the entourage came to Silver Creek, and Garet pulled the dun up beside the buggy.

'Welcome home, Laura.'

For a moment the sunlight reflecting from the light snow-cover blinded her. But then she saw the house. A real house standing on the small knoll above the creek, surrounded by corrals and fences, and a bunkhouse. Her home.

She could not believe her eyes.

'Oh, Garet. It's so . . . it's wonderful!'

She exclaimed over each new discovery as they approached the house, where Will, Wont and Travis rushed out to meet them, followed by Ness Havelock.

Rita jumped from the buggy and ran to him.

Ness greeted everyone, but his smile was for Rita alone.

'There's one thing a husband is supposed to do,' Garet said. 'Carry his wife across the threshhold of their new home.' Will hurried to open the front door. Garet picked Laura up in his arms and carried her into the H-Cross ranch house.

'Welcome home,' he repeated, lightly kissing her lips.

'Oh, Garet. Look!' Laura exclaimed. A table of long planks set up at one side of the room was laden with the haunch of beef, roasted over an oak fire in a makeshift fire-pit out back, and other foods and baked goods. Kettles and pots steamed atop the stove, tended by Dan Travis.

The others thronged into the house, and Garet shouted for their attention.

'Welcome to the H-Cross ranch, my friends,' he said. 'There is food and drink aplenty. Help yourselves.'

The afternoon turned into a fiesta with dancing to music by the *vaqueros* playing guitars they had stowed in the first wagon. Rita playfully insisted on teaching Ness to dance, and Laura danced as best she could with Garet, Miguel, Will and Dan, while Wont refused to try. Laura's joy infected everyone. Even the big brindle dog stoically suffered the attentions of the children from Rancho Pilar.

Late in the afternoon the Pilars took their leave. Don Fernando promised that the next Christmas fiesta would take place at Rancho Pilar. Ness would drive the buggy with Rita by his side and his horse tied on behind.

'Your friendship means the world to me,' Laura told Rita. 'I could never have made it through without you.'

The friends embraced, tears of joy welling.

Garet shook the hands of Don Fernando and Miguel.

'*Amigos*, you are welcome here any time.' To Ness he said: 'Little brother, I wish you good luck.'

'I hope I won't need it,' Ness replied, glancing at Rita waiting for him in the buggy.

After the Pilars and Ness had left, the H-Cross men retired to the bunkhouse. Garet and Laura stood alone in front of their new house.

'It's a good house, Laura,' Garet said. 'Havelock-built just for . . . the three of us. We'll be happy here. Merry Christmas, honey.'

'Merry Christmas, Garet. You. The house. Everything is perfect.'

'And come February,' Garet added, tenderly embracing her. 'We'll have our perfect baby.'

Once more, Garet Havelock took his wife in his arms and carried her across the threshhold into the H-Cross ranch house.